grace under
pressure

Faithgirlz!™ Backpack Bible
My Faithgirlz!™ Journal

The Blog On Series
Grace Notes (Book One)
Love, Annie (Book Two)
Just Jazz (Book Three)
Storm Rising (Book Four)
Upsetting Annie (Book Six)

Nonfiction
No Boys Allowed: Devotions for Girls
Girls Rock: Devotions for You
Chick Chat: More Devotions for Girls
Shine On, Girl!: Devotions to Keep You Sparkling

Check out www.faithgirlz.com

faiThGirLz!

grace under pressure

DANDI DALEY MACKALL

zonderkidz

ZONDERVAN.com/
AUTHORTRACKER
follow your favorite authors

The children's group of Zondervan

www.zonderkidz.com

Grace Under Pressure
Copyright © 2007 by Dandi Daley Mackall
Illustrations © 2007 by The Zondervan Corporation

Requests for information should be addressed to:
Grand Rapids, Michigan 49530

Library of Congress Cataloging-in-Publication Data

Mackall, Dandi Daley.
    Grace under pressure / by Dandi Daley Mackall.
        p. cm. -- (Blog on! ; 5)
    Summary: Gracie wants to lure her absentee mother home for Thanksgiv-
ing with a front page feature in the school's newspaper, only to find getting the
interview is a lot harder than she thought.
    ISBN-13: 978-0-310-71263-3 (softcover)
    ISBN-10: 0-310-71263-7 (softcover)
    [1. Mother and child--Fiction. 2. Interpersonal relations--Fiction. 3. Journal-
ism--Fiction. 4. High schools--Fiction. 5. Schools--Fiction. 6. Christian life--Fic-
tion.] I. Title. II. Series: Mackall, Dandi Daley. Blog on series ; bk. 5.
    PZ7.M1905Gru 2007
    [Fic]--dc22   2006015143

Art direction: Laura Maitner-Mason
Illustrator: Julie Speer
Cover design: Karen Phillips
Interior design: Pamela J.L. Eicher

Illustrations used in this book were created in Adobe Illustrator
The body text for this book is set in Cochin Medium

Printed in the United States of America

07 08 09 10 11 12 • 10 9 8 7 6 5 4 3 2 1

1

THAT'S WHAT YOU THINK!

by Jane

NOVEMBER 20

SUBJECT: I'M GETTING MY BIG BREAK!

This is it! My big chance. And I am not going to blow it. Not even if it means bottling up my sarcasm and anger and frustration. (Anybody want a really full bottle of SAF—sarcasm, anger, frustration?) I'll even force myself to smile and act interested, awestruck maybe. I can do this.

If you've been reading my blog for the last few months, you know I'm part of the vast media machine that supposedly runs our world: I blog. Obviously. But I also do my thing on the Typical High newspaper. As in most high schools, the upperclassmen get the best assignments. Since I'm the invisible sophomore on our newspaper staff, I get the leftover stories. All year I've been looking for my big break.

Now I have it. An assignment that could end up on page one with my byline.

What is this potentially groundbreaking front-page story? War? Famine? The environment? Crime? Politics?

None of the above.

No, the sad truth is that if you want to be on the front page of the Typical High News, you must be an athlete. Therefore it follows that if you want to write a front-page feature, you write about athletes. I volunteered to do an interview with our star wide receiver (whatever that is), hereafter referred to as "Wide Man." How sad is that? Sad, but not as sad as the fact that Wide Man has blown me off every time I've tried to talk to him.

That's not just sad. That's pathetic.

Grace Doe stopped blogging and glanced over her shoulder for the hundredth time. *That's What You Think!* was still an anonymous website, so it was crazy to be blogging in the *Shark* office, nerve center for Big Lake High School's student newspaper. But since it was Friday, she was the only one still there. Besides, she couldn't sit around all day doing nothing except waiting for football practice to end. How much practice did it take to knock each other down anyway? Her little brothers did it all the time, and they couldn't even *say* "football."

Gracie wouldn't leave, though. Not until she got her interview. She was going to talk with John Murphy, big-deal wide receiver, if it killed her. Or him.

A door swooshed open at the end of the hall, and some guy let out a whoop! Mass male laughter followed, accompanied by the thunder of football cleats.

Finally! Gracie logged off fast, grabbed her pack and reporter's notebook, and tore out to the hall.

She could smell them before she saw them. Coach must have worked the guys hard. A mass of bodies charged up the hall, heading right toward her. Gracie stood her ground. She was Lady Liberty in the New York Harbor, unmoved, in control. Guys elbowed and shoved each other, shouting and grunting.

Gracie leveled her gaze at the wad of football players. In their practice sweats, it was hard to tell them apart. They were all so ... so big. At 5'5", 120 pounds, she'd never considered herself especially little, until now.

Then she saw him. How could she have missed him? John Murphy was the tallest guy on the team. Gracie whipped out her notebook and jotted "Tall, blond, lean like a runner." She lowered the notebook to her side as they got closer and closer. The ground shook with the weight of them. *How many guys did it take to make a football team?* Old lightbulb jokes popped into her mind. *It takes one player to kick the football and ten to smack him on the backside and tell him what a great job he did.*

They were only a few feet away now. Grace didn't budge. She would get her interview and see her byline on page one, even if it meant cleat marks on her face as they trampled her.

"John!" she called. "Murphy!"

The leaders of the pack rushed past her. "Wide Man" towered toward the back of the mob.

"John Murphy!" she shouted. She could see his eyes, with irises like brown thumbprints.

They were laughing as they closed in around her. She couldn't breathe. Not without gagging anyway. Somebody bumped her from the left. She staggered and was spun around on the right.

Snippets of conversation floated to her as the bodies passed: " ... when I caught that pass! Sweet!" "If he thinks I'm going to — " " ... guy's a loser, man!" "Good lookin'-out, dude!" "We'll kill 'em Saturday!" "Got that right!"

They were past her now. Even Wide Man. Gracie screamed at their backs. "Hey! John Murphy! Stop! Murphy!" She cried out as loud as she could. Didn't they hear her? Didn't they see her? For a second, she wished she'd borrowed an outfit from Storm, her friend and fellow blogger. She could have used one of Storm's wild, colorful getups instead of wearing her standard-issue black pants and camouflage jacket. For once in her life, Gracie *wanted* to be noticed.

Nate, one of Annie's old boyfriends, turned and squinted in Gracie's direction. Annie wrote a love-advice blog on *That's What You Think!* Gracie had watched Annie expertly dump Nate after he cheated on her. Without stopping, Nate nodded at Gracie, then called up to Murphy, "Hey, Murphy! Somebody's calling you, man!"

Murphy stopped. Gracie felt her heart speed up, as if someone had raced her engine. She clutched her notebook to her chest and waved. Then she started toward him.

Murphy dropped his gym bag, reached inside, and came out with what looked like his cell phone. He flicked it open, frowned at it, then flipped it shut. "Nah, must be somebody else's. Nobody's calling me."

Wide Man disappeared into the locker room, but the words echoed through the halls and slammed into Grace Doe over and over again: *Nobody's calling me.*

Nobody...

Nobody...

Nobody...

2

Gracie stared after Murphy and the other jocks.

I should storm that locker room and demand to be heard! she thought. *See if they can hear "Nobody" then.*

But she couldn't move. Her feet were glued to the concrete floor.

"Move along!" Coach Ramsey shouted, inches from her ear. Gracie hadn't even heard him coming.

"No football groupies," he said. "I've told you girls—"

She spun around. "Groupies? Me?" Gracie had to mentally push the cork back into her bottle of anger. "I'm writing an article for—"

"Of course you are. Now, scoot."

Gracie took a deep breath and started counting, but she knew she'd never make it to ten. She shot up a quick prayer instead.

"It's almost dinnertime," Coach said. "Won't your mother be wondering where you are?"

"What?" Gracie glanced at her watch. He was right. It was so late! How could she have been waiting that long? She'd asked her mother to phone her from Europe at suppertime. Plus, with the crazy time zone in Paris, Victoria never seemed

to know what time it was back in Big Lake, Ohio. Gracie's
mom preferred to be called "Victoria," even by her daughter.
Gracie hadn't talked to her in weeks. They'd e-mailed and
IM-ed. But she wanted to hear Victoria's voice, to talk to her
in person. And now, she might have blown the whole article
and missed the call. For nothing.

"I have to go!" she announced.

Coach shouted something: "No fun in the fall!" Or maybe,
"Don't run in the hall!"

But Gracie was already down the hall with one foot out the
door.

Once outside, she poured on speed, crossing the school
lawn. Leaves crunched underfoot. The ground was soft from
day-old rain that probably should have been snow. *Please don't
let her call before I get there,* she prayed. Grace Doe didn't like
feeling desperate. *The call isn't really a big deal, God,* she prayed,
reigning in the desperation. *But I would like to talk to her.*

Halfway across Jackson Street, Gracie remembered she
wasn't going home. Making a one-eighty, she raced back
and turned north for the cottage. It was Victoria's cottage,
although she was rarely in it. Victoria could remember the
cottage phone number, so that's where she'd call. She was
always losing Gracie's cell and her home number. Or maybe
Victoria had a mental block against Gracie's real home, where
Gracie lived with her dad and stepmom.

Wiping her feet on the mat, she used both hands to open
the big oak door to the cottage. It wasn't locked. She stopped
in the doorway and listened. No ringing phone.

Mick, Gracie's little stepsis, looked up from the computer.
She was only twelve, but it was Mick's genius that kept *That's*

What You Think! running. And it was Mick's faith that seemed to hold the motley group of bloggers together as a team.

"Hey, Gracie!" Mick scooted back in her chair.

"Anybody call, Mick? For me?" Gracie dumped her pack next to the plush, white couch and wriggled out of her jacket.

"Annie called. She finished her 'Professor Love' column and has it on disk. You can pick it up if you stop by Sam's Sammich Shop tonight. Annie's working for her mom."

Gracie nodded. Annie Lind's column got the most hits on their blog. "I can stop by the shop later. But I'm bagging at the grocery store tomorrow, so I can't stay late. Saturday before Thanksgiving? Not going to be pretty."

"Plus," Mick added, "we've got the blog meeting first thing in the morning."

How could she have forgotten a blog meeting? Gracie crossed the room to the desk. "Are you sure nobody else called? Was the answering machine on?"

Mick's eyebrows lowered so far that her Cleveland Indians baseball cap inched over her glasses and her ponytail raised an inch. "You okay, Gracie?"

"Me? Why wouldn't I be?" Her response was automatic. Gracie knew she could tell Mick anything, but some things were better kept private, even from Mick. Gracie had asked her mother to call because she wanted to invite her to Big Lake for Thanksgiving. She and Victoria used to celebrate their birthdays on Thanksgiving, and it had been Gracie's favorite holiday. She wanted that again. But it wasn't Mick's problem. Why should she make Mick feel bad about something that didn't have anything to do with her?

"So," Gracie said, making herself sound more cheerful than she felt, "you done with the computer yet?"

Mick turned over the chair. "All yours. I've got homework anyway."

Gracie logged on and checked her e-mails. Lots of junk, a few website comments she could sort through later, a bunch of questions for Professor Love. Nothing from Victoria. Maybe that was good. At least Victoria hadn't canceled. Besides, there was still plenty of time for her to call. Gracie could blog to pass the time while she waited.

THAT'S WHAT YOU THINK!
by Jane

NOVEMBER 20

SUBJECT: LIFE'S WAITING ROOM IS EVERYWHERE

I have a rep as a keen observer. I read people. I work at it, taking notes as I skulk through the halls of Typical High. That's where I get most of my material for this blog.

Some of you write in to say that you stink at reading people. Others e-mail that they can never pick up on gestures or body language the way I do. But I'll bet that everyone reading this can tell when someone's waiting. Think about it. People do funny things when they're waiting:

- *If you see a man suddenly thrust out his arm, then jerk it back to check his watch, he's probably waiting on another man. Odds of this increase if said man is standing robot stiff.*

- *A guy waiting on his long-term girlfriend tends to sigh in big huffs and rub the back of his neck.*
- *A guy waiting on a first date may pace and press his lips together.*
- *Middle-aged men drum their fingers on the table.*
- *Middle-aged women tap their toes.*
- *Pacing, hand-wringing, head-holding, gawking—all possible signs of people waiting on people.*
- *Futile cell-phone checks or land-phone stare-downs are, of course, dead giveaways that somebody's waiting for a phone call.*

Gracie stopped blogging and stared at the phone on the desk, willing it to ring. Victoria called it a "Princess Phone." Pure white, it matched everything else in the white stucco cottage with big wooden beams. Victoria had brought in a designer from London to make the cottage look English.

Gracie glanced at the oak-framed wall clock. If Victoria were going to call, she would have called by now. Still, Gracie couldn't stop staring at the stupid phone and the soundless clock.

"Was Victoria supposed to call?" Mick asked softly.

"What?" Startled, Gracie turned to face her sister.

Mick hopped up on the edge of the desk and stared down at Gracie. "Something's bugging you. Is it your mom?"

Gracie sighed, then nodded. Somehow, admitting it made it feel worse, like poking a hole in the frustration bottle. The steam spit out.

"Did Victoria say she'd call you today?" Mick repeated, her eyes full of a sympathy Gracie couldn't handle.

Gracie shrugged, trying to make light of it. "It's probably the time difference between here and Paris. Or Vienna. Wherever."

Mick chewed her bottom lip, the way she did when she wanted to say more. "I'm sorry, Gracie. Why was she calling?"

Mick and Gracie had lived under the same roof for three years, long enough for Mick to know that Victoria never just called to talk. "I asked her to call me," Gracie admitted. "When we were instant messaging. I just ... I just had something I wanted to ask her. That's all. No big deal, Mick." Gracie could almost feel herself pulling away from Mick.

But Mick wouldn't let it go. "Why don't you call her?"

Gracie shrugged. "If she calls, then I know it's a good time to talk. I was thinking about asking her to come home for Thanksgiving."

"That's a great idea!" Mick exclaimed. "Mom would think it's cool."

Gracie thought about the time two Thanksgivings ago, when Victoria had spent the whole day with Gracie's new, blended family. Dad had been against the idea. But Lisa, Mick's mom, talked him into it. Lisa had done all the cooking. Somehow, she'd managed to keep everybody from feeling too weird, although Gracie remembered Dad's sigh of relief when Victoria left at the end of the day.

"I wasn't going to ask Lisa until I knew Victoria could do it," Gracie explained. "Do you really think your mom would be okay with it?"

"You know Mom," Mick said, grinning. "She'd love it."

Gracie had to admit that Lisa Doe was one of a kind. Gracie knew she'd lucked out in the stepfamily department, although she realized it wasn't luck. God had been in on it all the way, even though Gracie had fought him like crazy in the beginning. But Mick and her big brother, Luke, had become more like Gracie's brother and sister than steps. Dad's and Lisa's twins were over a year old now, and Gracie couldn't imagine life without them.

"How long do you think Victoria can get away for?" Mick asked.

"I'm hoping she'll stay for Thanksgiving and maybe a few days after so we can celebrate our birthdays." Gracie felt funny talking about it. She hadn't even prayed much about it yet. Praying and talking made her hopes too real, and she didn't want to set herself up for disappointment.

Mick hopped off the desk. "Sweet! But tell me about the birthday thing again. I know you already had yours a few months ago. We celebrated."

"Duly noted," Grace said, turning the computer chair back over to Mick. "Who could ever forget such a party? Big Lake's still buzzing about it." The celebration had been in the Doe household on August 19, Gracie's real birthday. The only guests were Mick, Luke — under protest because he had a *real* party to go to — and the twins, who stuck their paws into the cake while Lisa was blessing it. Dad had arrived late, but was sorry about it.

"Okay. So it was a pretty lame party," Mick admitted. "But it *was* your birthday, right?"

Gracie nodded.

"Is Victoria's birthday on Thanksgiving? And you guys just combined celebrating?"

"Nope." This would take some explaining. "Hang on."
Gracie went to the kitchen and got them Cokes. Then she
began. "Victoria's birthday is February twenty-fourth. Mine
is August nineteenth. She never told anyone when her birthday was, and she never wanted it marked by a celebration.
My mother doesn't get older." Gracie laughed. She hoped this
wasn't coming off like Victoria was some kind of crazy person, because it wasn't like that.

Mick was nodding, like she understood. "I've heard a lot of
women hate their birthdays. But how come you couldn't have
yours on August nineteenth?"

"That would have been the same as counting down *her* age,
like announcing that her daughter was another year older
meant *she* was another year older."

"So you didn't get birthday parties when you were little?"
Mick asked.

"Victoria has this way of making you believe she's doing
the most exciting thing in the world for you, no matter what
it is. She used to put on the absolute best parties for me:
secret birthdays, with just us. And always on Thanksgiving
so we'd have an excuse if someone stopped over and caught
us celebrating. I thought it was the most wonderful idea in
the world. Of course, you gotta remember I was too young
to know better. And then she left. Dad had regular birthday
parties for me after that, when I reminded him. But I miss
Victoria's parties. Nobody celebrates like Victoria."

They were silent for a minute. Gracie's throat felt tight. The
last thing she wanted was to cry about her mom. Or to make
Mick feel sorry for her. This was why she never talked about
these things.

The phone rang.

Gracie jumped as if the ring were a gun shot. She couldn't talk to Victoria *now*.

Ring! Ring! Ring!

"Gracie!" Mick cried. "Answer it!"

But she couldn't. Her hand wouldn't reach for the phone.

Mick dove for it and jerked the receiver to her ear, just as the answering machine clicked on. "Hello? Hello?" she shouted. Mick stood stiffly, eyes misting over. The phone dropped away from her ear. Mick stared at it, as if she'd never seen a receiver before. "Gracie, she hung up."

3

"She'll call back," Mick said, her voice weak and shaky.

Gracie hated herself for freezing like that. If she hadn't been spilling her guts to Mick, she would have been in control of her emotions. And now Mick was about to lose it too. She should have left Mick out of it.

By sheer force of will, Gracie pulled herself together. She picked up a pen from the desk and stuck it into her pocket. "Don't be whack, Mick. It was probably somebody trying to sell us real estate or aluminum siding. I keep forgetting to send this number to the no-call list." She managed what she thought was a pretty convincing smile for Mick. "Do you mind uploading my blog?"

"Sure, Gracie," Mick said. "And if Victoria calls, I'll tell her to call your cell."

Gracie retrieved her jacket and grabbed her pack. "Yeah. Good idea." But Gracie knew that wasn't going to happen. "Tell Lisa I'll get something to eat at Sam's, okay? I better go get Annie's disk. Maybe I'll get lucky and Murphy will be there. I told you I was interviewing him for the paper, right? Anyway ..." She was talking too much. She could tell by the way Mick was staring at her. Gracie had one hand on the doorknob.

The phone rang.

Mick got it before the first ring stopped. "Hello?"

Gracie's heart lodged in her throat. She squeezed the doorknob.

Mick's face drooped. "Hi, Storm. No, we just … we just thought you might be someone else." Her gaze shot to Gracie. "That was you too, then? Yeah, we didn't make it to the phone in time. Sorry."

Gracie waved at Mick and opened the door. She needed to be outside. By herself. The temperature must have dropped twenty degrees, and a splash of icy wind slapped her face and made her eyes water.

"Gracie?" Mick called, one hand over the receiver. "Wait. We can talk."

But Gracie let the door sweep shut behind her. The last thing either of them needed was another heart to heart. *Take care of Mick,* Gracie prayed as she cut through backyards to get to Main Street. *And Victoria.* Gracie stopped praying. She didn't feel like having a heart to heart with God either. Not about Victoria. Not about herself. Not right now. She couldn't afford to get all sad and emotional. *Okay, God. Changing the subject here, all I'm asking for me is that you help me get that interview. Deal?*

She did need to get that interview with Murphy. She'd hoped to write the article over the weekend and turn it in on Monday, in case there were any rewrites.

And it wasn't like interviewing John Murphy was all Gracie had to do. She'd picked up extra hours at the grocery store since she needed cash for Christmas shopping. There was the blog to write, the website to run. She'd promised to research software for Jazz, who took care of graphics for *That's What You Think!*

On top of all that, there was school. Gracie's backpack grew heavier every day. Teachers seemed to think
Thanksgiving week was a good time to give a test or have a
project due. Probably their way of making sure kids actually
went to school Monday through Wednesday. But Gracie had
always been good at juggling things. She'd just have to keep
all those "balls" in the air.

Sam's Sammich Shop lit the whole block as Gracie hurried
up Main Street. The town hadn't been able to wait until after
Thanksgiving to start Christmas. Candy canes hung on light
posts. Sam had already framed her front window with multi-
colored lights.

Beach Boys music escaped as customers scurried in and
out. Annie's mom, Samantha, had managed to make her place
the favorite high-school hangout in Big Lake. She and Annie's
grandparents had decorated retro, with jukeboxes, portraits
of the Beatles, and everything '60s. Gracie walked in just as
the Beatles finished singing "Help!"

"Gracie! You came!" Annie Lind waved from behind the
counter and almost dropped the water glasses she was carrying. A customer at the counter covered his head as if he were
being bombed. "Give me fifteen minutes. Then I have a break
coming."

Gracie nodded. "You got it."

Annie's mom walked up to Gracie and squeezed her shoulder. "Good to see you, Gracie! Can I get you something?"

"Thanks, Mrs. — I mean, Sam," Gracie said, correcting
herself. Samantha Lind insisted they call her "Sam." "I'm
starving. Could I have the Lennon Burger with fries?"

"You bet!" Sam rushed off toward the kitchen.

Gracie caught Sam and Annie exchanging grins as they passed each other. They looked, and acted, more like sisters than mother and daughter. Both were tall, about five foot ten, with shiny, auburn hair and blue eyes. Annie's dad had died in a plane crash when Annie was a baby, but Sam still talked about him so much that Gracie used to think he was just off on a trip.

The booths were crammed full, so Gracie claimed a table in the back. Murphy was nowhere in sight, but a bunch of his teammates were chilling at a big table at the far end of the room. So there was still hope Murphy could show.

It would have been nice if Storm or Jazz had been around, but Gracie didn't really mind eating alone or sitting by herself. It gave her time to observe people. And to start her blog. Wishing she had a laptop, she opened her observation notebook and took out her pen. Maybe she could expand the theme of waiting she'd started at the cottage. What better place to watch people wait than right here? Restaurants: home of the *wait*ress and *wait*er.

. . . .
THAT'S WHAT YOU THINK!
by Jane
NOVEMBER 20
SUBJECT: THE WAITING GAME CONTINUES...

At this moment, I'm sitting at a table in a local hangout. People are waiting all around me. (In fact, I'm waiting for a burger and fries, but that's beside the point.) One particular scene has captured my attention. A specific type of waiting: The Waiting Game. I'll attempt to give you a play-by-play.

Hair Goddess sits at the table closest to the entrance, surrounded by her flock of lesser hair goddesses. She is the star and lead contestant of this Waiting Game. She leans forward, elbows on table, all the while shooting covert glances toward the front door. Lesser hair goddesses are chatting, and HG laughs lightly, insincerely, with them. A few guys make an appearance and are dismissed without so much as eye contact from HG. Her eyes never stop moving. Her gaze is pulled magnetically to the door every few seconds. Her lips roll in, disappear, then unroll into a pout. Said lips are so flexible, so athletic, she could audition for the "O-lip-ics."

Then two things happen. First, Hair Goddess lowers her head into her hands and stares at the table. Second, at this precise instant, who should walk in, but Slick, the smoothest operator in the Typical High senior class.* (See below for the watched-pot-never-boils phenomenon.)

Hair Goddess looks up. Her eyes betray her as they widen. Eyebrows arch. Back straightens. Conclusion: HG has been waiting for Slick.

The game continues. HG's head jerks away from Slick as he slips off his ear buds and approaches her table. For the first time, HG seems intensely interested in what the lesser hair goddesses at her table have to say.

The drama continues. As Slick passes the group he calls out a general, "Hey!" before joining his own species at another table.

The wait over, Hair Goddess' emotions run the gamut. Her shoulders sag (disappointment). She sniffs and bites her upper lip (sadness). Then her jaw tightens to biting position (anger). She puts her hand behind her head, then withdraws it, palm down. I'm thinking Slick better run for his life.

Then she changes. She pops a fry. As she chews, her body un-tenses. Her arms un-stiffen. I can see her pupils constrict. She glances in Slick's direction, eyes narrowed, as if to say, "Just you wait, Slick. Just you wait."

And the game goes on. . . .

"It's wild tonight!" Annie plunked down a plate overflowing with a giant burger and fries. "Can't take a break yet. Sorry, Gracie. I hate leaving you alone."

"Chill, Annie. I'm cool." Gracie took a bite of the burger. "This is all I need. Thanks."

"Annie! Annie!" A table of freshman guys waved like they were bringing in a plane for a landing. You didn't have to be an expert in body language to figure out they all had crushes on Annie.

"You better go," Gracie advised.

Annie got applause when she reached the freshman table. Gracie turned back to her notebook, remembering that she still had to write the footnote about boiling pots:

Waiting: Watching the Pot Boil

I don't know enough about cooking or physics to know if there's any truth to the old saying, "A watched pot never boils." But I'll admit that it sure seems that way. Take, for example, Hair Goddess' vigilant watch for Slick, who only arrived when she wasn't watching.

Or, take a fashionable white telephone sitting on a big oak desk. Recently, I conducted my own experiment. I stared at just such a phone, waiting for it to ring, willing it to ring. Watching. And watching.

No ring.

But guess what happens if I turn away? Or if I leave the room or even leave the house? I'll tell you what happens.

Not a single thing. It still doesn't ring.

Or the wrong person phones.

So what's the moral of this suspenseful story? It's that whether or not you watch the pot, it's not going to boil for you. And that's all there is to that.

Gracie shut her notebook. This would be one of those blogs she didn't post. Her notebook was filled with them.

"Ha! There really are pink elephants, you know! In parts of Africa the soil has all this iron it. So, like, an elephant takes a dust bath, and voila! The dust cakes pink, and you've got yourself a pink elephant!"

Gracie swung toward the door, grinning. Yup, there she was. That little information tidbit could only be coming from Storm Novelo. Storm's head was so full of trivia that facts spilled out whenever she opened her mouth, which was most of the time. Storm never had trouble coming up with material for her *That's What You Think!* trivia column.

If Gracie had needed proof that God was behind the blog team, Storm was it. She and Gracie were so different that only God himself could have brought them together. Unlike Gracie, Storm Novelo was the center of attention wherever she went. She might show up with purple hair one day and orange-streaked black the next. But that wasn't why she commanded attention. It was like the atmosphere changed when Storm walked into a room. You *had* to look.

Gracie started over to see her. Storm was wearing paisley green jeans with a purple sequined top. She'd told Gracie she was mestiza: part Mexican and part Mayan. Even when she dressed like this, ready for disco, Storm managed to look like a Polynesian princess.

Guys swarmed around petite Storm, towering over her. "You don't eat like a pig, Jason!" she was saying. "More like a shark, buddy. Those tiger sharks will eat anything they can get down their throats. Even other sharks!"

Gracie laughed. She was about to push her way through Storm's crowd of admirers when the door to the shop slammed open, and Gracie caught a glimpse of John Murphy.

Wide Man!

This time she was not going to let him get away.

4

Gracie waited until John Murphy squeezed in at the crowded jock table. The guys made so much noise that she had trouble making out which Beach Boys tune was playing on the jukebox.

"Gracie!" Storm waved and patted the empty stool next to her at the counter. Gracie waved back. "In a minute, Storm!"

She took a deep breath. *Okay, God. Now or never. Don't let me wimp out.* Gracie grabbed a chair from the next table, slid it beside Murphy, and plopped herself down. A few of the guys frowned at her briefly, then looked away. Made her feel like roadkill. Dead animals on the road are momentarily disturbing. But they're not *your* pets, so they really have nothing to do with you.

Murphy, however, didn't even acknowledge "roadkill" when he saw it. He was in the middle of some story. "I told him if he had a problem with it, call Coach."

The table burst into laughter. Gracie tried to join in. "Good one. Murphy, could I talk to you about — ?"

But Murphy had turned to Josh, who was launching his own story. "Did I tell you about the blonde I met at the mall?"

"*We* met at the mall!" another jock added.

27

Josh ignored the interruption. "I asked for her number. And I swear she was going to give it to me. But this giant, a mutant from a chemical experiment gone horribly wrong, walked up and put his arm around her shoulder."

The other jock jumped in. "Giant? That guy was half your size, man!"

Gracie raised her voice. "This will just take a few minutes, Murphy."

"I know who you're talking about!" Murphy exclaimed. "No lie! Long blonde hair down to — "

"Murphy?" Gracie was on the edge of a shout now. She tried to pull back to conversational. "Who is she? Maybe I know her?"

Murphy ignored her. He took a long sip from Josh's root beer.

"Hey! Get your own, man!" Josh punched his arm.

Murphy took another drink, which earned him Josh's elbow in his side. Murphy returned the favor.

They're as bad as the twins, Gracie thought. "Murphy!" No response. "MUR-phy!" Louder that time. "**MURPHY-Y-Y-Y!**"

The shop went silent, except for the screech of chairs as people turned to stare. To stare at *her*. Time had frozen solid. Grace Doe was no longer that dead raccoon on the side of the road. She was the bull in the china shop, the elephant at the ballet.

Glancing from one jock to the other, she read their expressions: a mixture of disgust, pity, and fear. This was a horror movie, and Gracie was the star.

The cold silence was broken by the *click clack* of high heels crossing the room. Purple and red strappy heels. With giant bows. Gracie saw this because her head was locked in down position, staring at the floor as the shoes entered her field of vision.

"That scream was so tight, Grace!" Storm exclaimed. "Did you guys know that Toby Teneca holds the record for the loudest and longest scream? At least he did until tonight. Way to go, Gracie! Nice exhibition!"

Gracie didn't move. The shop was still quiet, except for Storm.

"Maybe you guys failed to realize," Storm said, strutting around the table of jocks, "that, counting Gracie, there are thirteen of you at this table. Thirteen! And it's Friday. True, not Friday the thirteenth. Nope. No Friday the thirteenth this month. Why, you ask?" She addressed the crowd, with a little 360-degree twirl. "Because November didn't start on a Sunday! Months that begin on a Sunday will always have a Friday the thirteenth. So beware of next month!"

Gracie dared to look up. Now the guys were smiling, staring at Storm instead of her. A wave of gratitude shot through her.

"Triskaidekaphobia," Storm continued, reaching over and taking hold of Gracie's arm. "Fear of the number thirteen. I noticed that none of you guys wears that particular number on those unfortunately colored costumes you play football in."

Gracie let herself be lifted from the chair.

"Ah, football." Storm shook her head at the guys, who looked hypnotized. "Bet you don't know why the football used to be called a pigskin. Because footballs used to be made of pigs' bladders, wrapped up neatly in pigs' skin. That is so full of nastiness, I can't even talk about it!"

She backed away from the table, and Gracie backed away with her.

"But seriously," Storm explained, "I'm afraid Gracie's scream didn't quite beat Toby's record. You need more practice, girlfriend. To the kitchen with you!" She tugged on Gracie's arm, then smiled back at the guys. "As you were, gentlemen! And if you hear screams coming from the kitchen, that will be Gracie practicing. Carry on!"

Gracie was in the kitchen before she found her voice again. "Thanks." She could have said so much more. She'd never needed rescuing before, not like this. Storm had ridden to her rescue as surely as if she'd been on a white horse. "Thanks, Storm. I ... I guess I lost it."

"What were you thinking?" Storm snapped. "I couldn't believe it when I saw you sit down with those guys! Then that scream. What was that about?"

Annie put an arm on Gracie's shoulder. "Do you *like* him, Gracie? Is that it?"

Gracie swung around to Annie. "Like him? Murphy? Are you kidding? He's horrible!"

"So why the play?" Storm asked.

Gracie didn't like letting the whole world in on her problems. But it was a little late for privacy now. "I need an interview with Murphy. For the *Shark*. They might run it on the front page. Turns out he's some big-deal football star with college scouts coming out to watch him."

"True dat!" Annie agreed. "He'll get a scholarship anywhere he wants to go."

"So your plan was to interview him at the top of your lungs?" Storm asked.

"I've been trying all week to get this interview, but he ignores me. I'm out of time, Storm. I have to write the piece this weekend." Gracie noticed Annie's grandfather flipping burgers at the big grill.

Mr. Lind smiled over at her. "Hello, Grace. That's a nice jacket you have there. Had one like it myself once. In the army."

Gracie was grateful that he was acting as if she hadn't made a complete idiot out of herself. "Hey, Mr. Lind. Thanks. Army Surplus."

"So what's the problem, Gracie?" Annie asked, tearing out a page from her waitress pad and sticking it above the grill. "Murphy's cool. Did you ask him to give you an interview?"

"Ask him to give me an interview? Now there's an idea. Why didn't I think of that?" Gracie felt bad as soon as she said it. "Sorry, Annie. It's just that — yes — I asked him. And asked him. And asked him."

"So we'll let Annie ask him for you," Storm suggested. "No guy can say no to Annie Lind."

Annie laughed and headed out to the shop. "Sure. Be right back."

"Wait!" Gracie called.

"Chill, Gracie." Storm put her hand on Gracie's arm. "Give her a minute. Then you can have your shot."

"But — " Gracie hated having everybody involved like this. She wanted to do this herself. She dashed out of the kitchen and started toward the jock table. But she froze. Gracie watched helplessly as Annie marched up to the guys and tapped the table, like she was knocking and waiting to be invited in.

They invited her.

Gracie couldn't hear what they were saying, but she could read the body language and gestures. It was all she needed.

Annie cocked her head to one side and tossed her hair. Gracie didn't quite understand what was going on. But by the looks of things, whatever Annie was doing was working. Murphy scooted to the edge of his chair and smiled up at her. He said something, then threw his head back and laughed.

Annie laughed too. But Gracie noticed her shoulders stiffen. One hand went to her waist, a sure sign of irritation, anger even. Gracie could tell that Annie was not enjoying this. It made her feel even worse.

Annie's eyes widened as she spoke. That meant she was pleading. This would be the part where she asked Murphy to give the interview. Gracie could hardly bear to watch.

Murphy pursed his lips together and shook his head slowly. It was a reluctant no.

Annie lowered her chin. Classic begging gesture. She hugged her arms, presenting a need to be rescued.

Apparently, it was all too much for Murphy. He sighed. Then, smiling up at Annie, he shrugged and nodded. This got him a huge grin from Annie. She held up one finger, then dashed back behind the counter.

"You did it," Gracie said. She had to admire Annie. Annie had accomplished in one minute what Gracie couldn't pull off in a week. "I owe you, Annie. Thanks."

Annie shrugged. "Don't worry about it, Gracie. Just get out there and get a fantastic interview!"

"Out *there*?" Gracie didn't know what she'd expected, but it wasn't interviewing Murphy out there, where she'd just made an idiot of herself.

"Don't you think the interview would go better if you got Murphy away from his buddies?" Storm suggested.

"Yeah!" Gracie agreed. *Like on another planet.*

Annie crooked her finger at Murphy, and he came trotting over. "You and Gracie can corner the last two stools for the interview," she said. "How's that?"

It was about as private as Gracie could hope to get at Sam's. "Um ... thanks," she said, trying to regain control. She pulled out her notebook and sat down, motioning Murphy to take the end stool. "Murphy, I appreciate you giving me your time. So, spell your name for me, okay?" She knew how to spell his name, but it was an old interviewing technique. Put the subject at ease by asking easy questions first. Now all she needed was a technique to put *her* at ease.

Murphy spelled his name and waited.

"Thanks," Gracie said. "You're a junior, right?"

"Mmm-hmm. Hey, do you know if Annie's seeing anybody?"

Gracie looked up from her notes. "Yeah. I mean, I'm not sure. She's kind of going out with this guy from our church, I think." It was hard to keep up with Annie's love life, but she'd been spending quite a bit of time with Dallas, a guy from Middleview, who went to their church.

"Anyway," she continued, moving into the real questions she'd prepared, "tell me what it's like being a star wide receiver."

"It's okay, I guess. I mean, I like it."

"Are you expecting to get a scholarship?"

"To a great school," he answered. But he didn't sound as excited as Gracie would have been.

"That must be the best feeling, to know that you'll be playing ball in college and getting an education for free?"

"I guess."

Gracie launched into the questions she'd written out beforehand. She asked him about his best game, but she also made him talk about his worst game. She'd designed several questions as hard hitting. "What do you think of Coach? Would you do anything differently if you were coaching the team?"

"I'd focus on teamwork, learning each others' strengths, and having fun. I wouldn't yell at the guys."

This answer was pretty interesting. Maybe even controversial. Gracie hoped so.

"Why wide receiver? Haven't you ever wanted to play a different position?"

Murphy seemed to think about that one before answering. "I've always been tall. And pretty fast. My dad thought I'd do best as wide receiver."

"Does he come to your games?"

Murphy laughed. "Are you kidding? My parents fight over who's my number-one fan and who's number-two fan. They haven't missed a game since I was five and Grandma died. They *live* for my games."

Gracie tried not to dwell on that answer, but she couldn't help wondering what it would feel like to have your parents cheer you on like that. She took pages of notes as she moved through the rest of her questions.

"Is that it?" Murphy asked when she'd flipped through her notebook to make sure she hadn't forgotten anything.

"I guess so. Thanks a lot, John." She stuck out her hand, and he shook it. Gracie wondered what kind of a guy John Murphy really was. Was he frontin' being bored? Did he love the game? Was he a nice guy, or not? She honestly didn't know.

5

Gracie hurried home to write up her interview notes while the details were fresh in her mind. She'd just started when Mick knocked, then came on into the bedroom.

"Hey, Gracie. Everything go okay at Sam's?"

"Sure, Munch," she answered. Sooner or later, Mick would hear about Gracie's scream and the interview and everything. But later would be better. Right now Gracie wanted to get going on the article. "Are you going to bed?"

"Yep. I'm beat. Night, Gracie."

Gracie got an idea for a lead and started typing it in when there was another knock on the door. This time it was Dad. She hadn't seen much of him all week. She knew he'd been working on a big ad account, something to do with pickles.

"I won't bother you," he said, sticking his head in. "Just wanted to say goodnight. Sorry I've been so scarce around here. But I closed the Bender account. They're running my ad in all the wholesaler trades."

"That's great, Dad." Hallway light framed his stocky silhouette, making him look like a thick shadow. For a second, Gracie wanted to run over and hug him, just to make sure he was real.

"Anyway," he said, yawning, "I'm sleeping in tomorrow. Night, honey."

"Night, Dad."

Gracie started writing again, but other thoughts kept bombarding her mind. She needed to finish her English essay. And read her history chapters.

She checked her cell again, wishing she'd stopped by the cottage and checked the answering machine, just in case.

Shoving telephones and answering machines out of her head, Gracie went back to her interview notes. But thoughts of Victoria kept surfacing and wrecking her concentration.

It was no use. Gracie clicked on her inbox to see if Victoria had left her a message. There was one from Jazz, saying she might stop over in the morning so they could walk to the blog meeting together.

But nothing from Victoria.

Gracie stared at the screen. Why couldn't Victoria remember to call when she said she would? They'd been really clear about the phone date, hadn't they? Or maybe … maybe they hadn't been so clear? Maybe Gracie had messed up the day. She'd saved all of Victoria's e-mails in a separate folder, transferring them from her old computer when she'd gotten a new one.

She clicked on the "Victoria" file. It didn't take long to find the e-mail she was looking for. No mistake. Victoria had agreed to call the cottage at suppertime on Friday. Today. Only she hadn't.

Gracie couldn't help scanning the messages in her Victoria folder until the letters blurred.

She squeezed her eyes shut. *God, I pray for Victoria. Would you mind reminding her that she promised to call me? And I'd really like*

it if she could get away from all her work there and come to Big Lake
for Thanksgiving. I know she's really busy and all. And I'm okay if it
doesn't work out and everything. Really I am. It's just —

She stopped praying. Sometimes, if she went too far with
a prayer, it could make her sad. And she didn't want that.
Gracie didn't want to let herself feel sad.

For curiosity's sake, she logged on to her Instant
Messenger. Gracie had never thought of herself as chatty. The
only person she IM-ed was her mom. Victoria, on the other
hand, had a list a mile long of her "chat buddies."

As soon as Gracie logged on, a message popped up: *Victoria*
is online. She was in a chat room.

Gracie waited. She didn't feel like chatting, especially with
other "buddies" in the room. But she couldn't help herself.
She pictured Victoria at the other end of cyberspace. She'd be
elegant, in a long, black evening gown, probably on her way
to somewhere important. Victoria was more beautiful than
Gracie would ever be.

She clicked to the chat room, but didn't enter. Instead, she
eavesdropped:

Handsome1:	*I'm not kidding you, Vic! You looked hot! The camera loves you.*
Victoria:	*You're sweet. I don't know. I should have asked tougher questions.*
Handsome1:	*Nobody was listening. Believe me. They were too stunned by your beauty.*
GTO4me:	*So, V, what do you say? You and me and my GTO, driving to the Riviera for Thanksgiving? Sun, fun, food?*

Victoria:	*Very tempting. I don't know.*
Handsome1:	*Forget that! Come away with me, cherie! I will show you a France you will never forget. Moonlight walks on the beach.*
GTO4me:	*But with me, picture a spin along the beach in my GTO! We can stay at my family's castle.*
Handsome1:	*Castles are cold! I am warm!*
GTO4me:	*Hey! I knew this lovely lady before you!*
Victoria:	*Gentlemen, please! You boys are dolls—you know that—but I've got so much work to catch up on. As much as I hate to, I must decline your gracious invitations. Still, it's nice to be wanted.*

Gracie couldn't take it. She could hear Victoria's light-hearted voice behind the printed words. Nice to be wanted? *Everybody* wanted Victoria. And nobody, nobody wanted her more than Gracie. Before she could stop herself, she typed:

I agree. It must be nice to be wanted. Maybe wanted enough to have somebody call you when they say they will. Especially when you were hoping that this somebody might actually consider coming home once in a while. Like, maybe to celebrate Thanksgiving and birthdays. I wonder what that feels like—to be wanted.

Gracie was shaking as she shut down the computer without logging off, something she never did. Her words to Victoria replayed in her head as she lay awake in bed.

When Gracie woke up the next morning, her first thought was a hope that last night's chat room had been a dream. More like a nightmare. But she knew better. Gracie had never said, or written, things like that to Victoria. What if Victoria couldn't handle it? What if she got so angry she'd never write again?

Gracie felt sick thinking about it. Dragging herself out of bed, she bumped her bedside table. Something fell to the floor. When she picked it up, she realized it was the disk Annie had given her at Sam's. Gracie hadn't even looked at it, and the blog meeting started in an hour.

It took ten minutes and a cold shower to wake up. Then she popped in Annie's CD. Since she hadn't logged off of IM, the symbol popped up as an ugly reminder of last night's chat room. Gracie didn't want to know how Victoria had responded.

The blog meeting started in an hour. Gracie needed to focus on the website. Willing herself to put Victoria out of mind, she read what was in front of her on the screen:

·
THAT'S WHAT YOU THINK!

PROFESSOR LOVE

Dear Professor Love,

My boyfriend broke up with me, and I can't stop crying. He dumped me. Turns out he's been dating somebody else behind my back. And still, after a horrible week, I feel sad and miss him. It's all I can do to pretend to be okay. What's wrong with me?

—Dumpster Dana

Dear Dana,

Hey, it's okay to cry, get mad, feel hurt. That's what people do when they break up! Don't be so hard on yourself. What you're feeling is normal. Just be sure you let out your feelings in a safe place—with God, family, and friends. They'll help you move on.

—Love, Professor Love

Dear Professor Love,

I'm so mad at my boyfriend. He forgot our anniversary of the day we met. Then he forgot our anniversary of our first date. Then he forgot our anniversary of the first time he told me he loved me. What is up with that????

—MemoryGirl

Dear MemoryGirl,

Does your boyfriend's forgetfulness surprise you? Silly you. Remember two things, and you won't get so upset: 1) Men forget. 2) Men forget everything. Why else do you think they have to have all those instant replays?

—Love, Professor Love

Dear Professor Love,

I'm tall. Really, really tall, okay? But why does every girl I meet have to ask me if I play basketball? Short guys do the same thing. What can I do?

—TallGuy

Dear TallGuy,

I hear you! I'm tall too—for a girl. Here's an idea. Why don't you start asking those "shorties" if they play miniature golf?

And besides, God made you tall. Be happy in your tall-ness!

—Love, Professor Love

Dear Professor Love,

I'm writing you because I don't know what 2 do 2 help my older sister. She wants 2 go back 2 her old boyfriend. He was a player and treated her lousy when they were going together. That's Y she finally broke up with him. Now she wants 2 go back with him, and I know it's just because she hasn't found anybody else. I've tried logic and telling her she should learn 2 be happy on her own and that she doesn't need a boyfriend 2 make her happy. But I need a Professor Love line that will stick with her. Can you help?

—Sis

Dear Sis,

Good for you! Great logic, and you're right. Your sister needs to learn how to be happy without a guy. It's the only way she'll ever be really happy with one. So, you've already given great advice. (In fact, if I quit, do you want a job as Professor Love?)

But since you want a comeback for her, try this: Taking your crummy boyfriend back is like buying your own junk at your garage sale.

— Love, Professor Love

Gracie thought about how much Annie had grown in the few weeks she'd been blogging. She'd always been funny. But now she sometimes went deeper. God was cropping up more and more in Annie's advice columns.

While she got dressed, Gracie listened to the jungle downstairs. The twins had been in wild-animal mode all week. This morning it sounded like elephants and monkeys.

Gracie took the stairs two at a time. She wanted to get to the cottage first and set up for the meeting. "Morning, all!" she called, as she strode into the kitchen.

Lisa was on hands and knees, wiping up something that looked like Cream of Wheat. She smiled up at Gracie. Even covered in lumpy white stuff, Lisa was cute — five feet, one hundred pounds of spunk. "And good morning to you, Gracie. Your brothers are in rare form. You missed the Cream of Wheat slingshot competition."

Mick dashed over from the sink with a handful of paper towels. She was already dressed in sweats and a Cleveland Indians sweatshirt. "Hey, Gracie!" Kneeling beside Lisa, she finished cleaning the mess. "I'm meeting Ty to practice my curve this morning. But don't worry. I'll be at the blog meeting. If you get there before me, pull up the site and see if you like the verse I posted."

"What can I do to help here?" Gracie crossed over to where Daniel and David sat, banging on each other's high chair trays. She kissed the top of their heads.

"More!" David demanded.

Gracie kissed him again. He tasted like orange juice. She didn't ask.

"No, me!" Daniel yelled, shoving David's tray.

Gracie kissed him too. He tasted sour. Milk maybe? "Hey, guys. Do me a favor and take it easy on your mom today, will you?"

As an answer, the boys exploded into animal sounds that could have been anything from a lion to a cow.

Gracie shrugged. "I tried."

Lisa grinned over at her from the sink, where she was washing out a once-white toddler T-shirt. "Just tell me it's a phase," Lisa pleaded. "Or that they both woke up on the wrong side of the bed. They've been fighting all morning."

"You're kidding." Usually the boys banded together to fight the rest of the world.

"Is Luke still asleep?" Mick asked, peeling a banana.

"Far as I know," Lisa answered. "So's your dad. Hmm ... The two big men in the house sleep in, while we try to handle the two little men in the house. What's wrong with this picture?"

Suddenly, Daniel started screaming. Not a *give-me-a-cookie* scream, but a *help-I'm-scared* scream. He kicked so wildly in his chair that Gracie dove to steady it.

Then David screamed even louder than his brother.

Lisa was there in a flash. "What's the matter? It's okay, guys." But Gracie could tell she was worried. Something was wrong.

Daniel twisted in the chair while Lisa removed the tray. Gracie did the same for David. David buried his head against her neck while Daniel writhed in Lisa's arms.

"What is it?" Mick asked, stroking Daniel's hair. He pointed out the window and screamed again.

"Nah-a-a-ah!" David cried. Then Daniel joined him.

"Nah-a-a-ah!"

"At least they're agreeing on something," Gracie offered. She felt bad, though. They were genuinely scared. "I think they saw something outside."

Lisa peeked out the window, then hoisted David onto one hip and took Daniel from Gracie, balancing him on her other hip, as if she were toting two footballs to the goalpost. "Come on, boys. There's nothing to be afraid of outside. Mama will show you."

"Let me take Daniel," Mick said, opening the door and reaching for her brother.

"I've got 'em," Lisa assured her.

"You sure?" Gracie asked. Cold air swooshed in. Lisa was still in her slippers and robe, although the boys had their wooly, footed PJs on.

"Back in a sec!" Lisa zipped outside into the gray fog and disappeared behind the chubby pines.

"Maybe we should go after them," Mick said.

Gracie was about to agree, when at the window she saw a tiny burst of light explode, then disappear. "Mick, did you see that?"

"See what?"

Gracie looked hard at the place she'd seen the light. The gray sky seemed to hover close to the ground making it hard to see. Then the flash of light came again. And again.

6

Gracie had her hand on the doorknob when the door opened. In walked Lisa, still toting the twins. Behind her came Jasmine Fletcher, "Jazz" to the blog team.

"Look who I found," Lisa said. Skillfully, she shuffled the twins back into their high chairs.

"Jazz!" Mick exclaimed, glancing over Jazz's shoulder. Gracie figured she was looking for Ty, Jazz's little brother.

"What were you doing out there, Jazz?" Gracie asked.

Jazz held up a camera. That explained the flashes. "Your hickory tree is so tight without leaves. Can't believe I never noticed the shape of the trunk and the main limbs."

"So you were taking pictures of our hickory?" Gracie asked.

"Among other picture-worthy items in our yard," Lisa added. "Like frost-covered dirt and dead flowers."

Jazz grinned. "It's my new art form."

"I thought so," Lisa said, pouring herself a cup of coffee. "Would you like some breakfast, Jasmine?"

"No thanks, Mrs. Doe." Jazz turned to Mick. "Hey, Mick, I almost forgot. Ty said to meet him behind the cottage so you guys could practice."

47

"Thanks!" Mick took the last bite of her banana and dropped the peel in the under-the-sink trash can. "I'm outta here. See you guys at the cottage."

Jazz unzipped her sleek black jacket, so her electric blue turtleneck popped out. Knee-high boots covered black stretch pants. She'd probably designed and made everything she had on. Gracie thought Jazz looked like a modern dancer. No matter what she wore, she looked cool.

"I should be taking more pictures of the boys," Lisa said, glancing back at the twins. They were locked in a stare-down. "I keep forgetting to use the camera. I hardly have any pictures of our family." She swallowed a gulp of coffee, then set it down on the table. "Jazz, would you take some pictures of the boys? Right now? Then I can get copies made and pay you for the film."

"It's a digital," Jazz explained. "No problem."

David snatched the spoon from Daniel's tray and cried, "Mine!"

Daniel returned the favor, grabbing David's spoon in his fist. "Mine!" Then they threw the spoons toward each other.

Jazz snapped pictures of the whole scene.

While Gracie downed a bowl of cereal and Lisa answered the phone, Jazz took shots of Daniel shaking David's arm, of David throwing food at Daniel, of David trying in vain to kick his brother's chair, and his brother succeeding in returning the kick.

Lisa came back to the kitchen. "So, how is the photo session coming along?"

"All finished," Jazz announced. "Only with all the violence, I don't think anybody under eighteen should be allowed to view these images."

As they left for the cottage, Gracie zipped her jacket against the fierce west wind. "Thanks for coming by early, Jazz."

"No sweat. I needed some outside shots to finish off my project."

"Your project?" Gracie was only half listening. Walking toward the cottage made her think of Victoria. And thinking of Victoria made her think of last night's chat room and the stupid, childish things she'd written.

"*My* art project?" Jazz said. "Hello? What are you doing anyway?"

Art project. Gracie stopped in the middle of the street.

"Gracie!" Jazz took her arm and pulled her to the other side of the street, as a pickup rolled by.

Gracie had totally forgotten about the assignment from art class. "When's it due?"

"You're kidding, right?" Jazz stopped smiling. "This Wednesday. Before the break. You seriously haven't started yet?"

Gracie shook her head. How had she forgotten? She'd always been good with juggling the balls in her life, keeping them in the air. "I dropped the ball, Jazz. I totally forgot we had a project due." Art was such an easy class. At least, most of the time. She wasn't good at anything in art, not like Jazz, who was great at everything. But nobody had trouble passing the class. "What am I going to do?"

"Gracie, this isn't like you."

"I know." She took a deep breath. She could handle this. She sure didn't need to get Jazz involved. Jazz had enough problems of her own. "It's okay. I'll come up with something.

Maybe I'll take pictures too. At least then I don't have to draw anything."

"Taking pictures isn't the same as the art of photography, you know," Jazz said, making them walk on.

"Not to mention the fact that I don't even own a camera." They were heading up the sidewalk to the cottage now. Gracie heard Mick and Ty out back, playing ball, even in this cold. "Don't worry about it," Gracie said, trying to sound like *she* wasn't worried. "I've got a couple of ideas." She dug out her key and unlocked the door. "Come on in. We need to talk about software."

Morning lit up the cottage, so they didn't need to flip on the lights. Jazz showed Gracie some software programs that might help with graphics on the website, and Gracie promised to make a decision before their next meeting.

"Let's check out what Mick's already loaded on the site," Gracie suggested, moving to the computer. She logged on to the homepage of *That's What You Think!*, and there was Mick's verse for the week:

"Come to me, all you who are weary and burdened, and I will give you rest. Take my yoke upon you and learn from me, for I am gentle and humble in heart, and you will find rest for your souls. For my yoke is easy and my burden is light." — Matthew 11:28–30

Gracie shook her head and inhaled. The beginning of a chuckle came out when she exhaled. Usually Mick's verses were right on the money, saying exactly what she was feeling. Not today.

"What?" Jazz pushed in behind her and read over her shoulder.

Gracie wanted to be careful. For a long time, Jazz hadn't liked the idea of putting anything from the Bible on the website. Lately, things had been changing. Jazz had come to a place where she admitted there was a God, a Creator she'd like to know better. As far as Gracie knew, Jazz still hadn't found her way to Christ. But Gracie was sure she'd get there, especially with Mick around.

Jazz stared at the screen. "Matthew was one of the disciples, right? Is that something he said? ' ... my burden is light'? I don't get it."

"It's something Jesus said," Gracie explained. "Matthew just wrote it down." She wished Mick would come in. Mick could have explained the verse and talked about Jesus in a way that wouldn't turn Jazz off. Gracie wanted to say something. But this verse wasn't it. Right now, her burden felt anything but light.

Finally, Jazz reached in and took over the mouse. "Let's see if Storm's got her column posted yet." They scrolled down until they found it:

•
THAT'S WHAT YOU THINK!

DIDYANOSE

I have to say that I'm tiring of readers who write in to call me "brainy" or say I must have a giant brain. Obviously, too many readers know too little about the brain.

Did you know?

- *The average human brain weighs 3 pounds.*
- *The largest human brain we know about was 5 pounds, and it wasn't Einstein's. His brain was smaller than average.*
- *Our brains make up about 2% of our body weight, but it uses about 20% of our energy.*
- *Elephant brains weigh about 13 pounds. No wonder an elephant never forgets.*

I've been noticing how nervous everybody's becoming the closer we get to Thanksgiving break, with all the work teachers pile on us. So that's made me think more about our nerves and emotions. Did you know that information travels in our nerves at speeds up to 268 miles per hour? No wonder we feel so knicked out all the time!

But why do we get so nervous, and what are we nervous about? Did you know the top three fears, in this order, are: 1) snakes; 2) heights; and 3) flying? Except for high-school guys: I think they're mostly afraid of brainy girls.

"Not bad," Gracie admitted. And it probably hadn't taken Storm more than a few minutes to come up with it.

"Hey." Jazz pointed to the phone. "You've got a message on your answering machine."

Gracie looked. She hadn't noticed the tiny red dot on the answering machine until this second. Now, she stared at the red light. It blinked on and off. On and off like an SOS signal.

7

"Aren't you going to check your messages?" Jazz asked, reaching for the answering machine.

"No! I mean, not now. It's probably just somebody selling magazine subscriptions." Gracie's chest felt like a flock of hummingbirds was trying to get out. She forced herself to keep cool. There was no way it was her mother, and she was not going to get pulled into hoping that it was. Besides, even if there were a message from Victoria, it wouldn't be a nice, motherly one. Not after the message Gracie had sent *her*. No way did Gracie want her friends in on the messy relationship she had with her mother. "Just leave it, Jazz. I'll erase it later."

The front door swung open, and Mick flew in. "I'm not late, am I?" She shed her coat, then her sweatshirt. It had started snowing, and Mick was soaking wet.

"Mick," Gracie said, "I can't believe you were playing ball in this weather."

"*I* can," Jazz muttered. "Ty's just as bad."

"Victoria's got all kinds of clothes back in the bedroom," Gracie said. "Go put on something dry."

Mick was already backing up to the entryway and taking off her shoes. "Are you sure, Gracie? Your mom won't mind?"

"Victoria? She doesn't even know what she's got in that closet. Go!"

Minutes later, Storm and Annie burst in. Storm was wearing her yellow raincoat, yellow hat, and yellow boots. Even her hair was in a yellow banana clip. "Is this typical Big Lake, Ohio, weather for this time of year?" Storm asked, kicking off her boots. "I'd like to know where global warming is when you really need it."

"I forgot this is your first winter in our fair land," Annie said, shedding her snow jacket. "Maybe if you dressed for a snowstorm, instead of a rainstorm, it would work better. Just a thought." Annie's own white silk jacket couldn't have been very warm or waterproof, but Gracie supposed it was totally fashionable. "Last year we got two feet of snow for Thanksgiving," Annie added.

"*Now* you tell me," Storm muttered. "And I've already unpacked my bags."

"Hey, guys!" Mick called. She twirled, modeling a pink Mohair sweater that was four sizes too big and definitely not Mick the Munch. "Like it?" She stopped as she swirled past the desk. Her eyes grew big. "Gracie! There's a message on the — !"

Gracie moved between Mick and the phone and gave her sister a look meant to silence. "It's okay, Mick. I'm going to erase the messages later. We need to get started."

Gracie called the meeting to order and tried to keep the discussions down to business. Usually, she loved blog meetings, when they brainstormed themes and developed new ideas. But her mind kept wandering to the answering machine. She wanted to get the meeting over so she could listen to the message. Alone.

"So," she said, after about twenty minutes of trying to keep everybody on track, "does that about do it?"

"Whoa! This is a first," Storm commented. "Grace Doe itching to bounce from a blog meeting?"

"I just thought we were done," she answered, trying not to sound defensive.

"I'm not done," Jazz said. "I don't have a cartoon this week because I've been waiting to see if we could get that new software."

Annie had curled up in her favorite easy chair next to the fire. "I could stay here all day. Gracie, did you pull off the e-mails for 'Professor Love'?"

"Rats! I meant to do it last night. Or this morning." She'd had it on her mind all week. She just hadn't gotten to it. It was starting to feel like the more things she did, the more things there were to do. "I'll e-mail them to your account today. Okay, Annie?"

Annie sighed. "I guess. But I could have started on them this morning. Next week's going to get crazy."

That was the understatement of the century. "Listen, guys," Gracie tried. "I've got to get to the grocery store."

"Be easy, Gracie!" Storm said, checking her watch. "We're on the same shift." She turned to Annie. "Can you drive us?"

Annie sighed again. "I suppose. I have to get over to the shop anyway. Mick, you coming?"

Mick glanced from Annie to Gracie. "Um ... yeah. Thanks. I told your mom I'd help out at the shop today. Gracie? You want us to go ahead without you?"

Gracie knew Mick was onto her. The Munch was trying to make it easier for her to stay behind and hear the messages.

That's what Gracie longed to do too. But she didn't want to act like it was a big deal. She forced herself to smile. "No way! And miss a chance to be chauffeured by Annie Lind? Let's bounce!"

They bundled up and left together. Gracie took one last look at the blinking red light of the answering machine and locked the door behind her.

"Right on!" Storm was saying to the tenth Big Lake Foods' customer who'd asked her about her all-yellow outfit. "The yellow *is* in honor of our sale on bananas, which I'm glad to see that you're taking advantage of, in spite of the usual pumpkin and turkey stockpile."

Gracie had expected the lines to be longer since everyone was doing Thanksgiving shopping. But the lines were about the same as any normally busy Saturday. The difference was in the carts, filled to overflowing.

"Did you know bananas are second cousins to lilies and orchids?" Storm asked the customer. "Bananas rock! Low fat, no cholesterol, no sodium!"

Tammy Jo, Storm's cashier, placed the bunch of bananas on the scale.

"Ooh!" Storm exclaimed. She closed her eyes. "TJ, let me guess! Nine bananas, right? One finger short of an official *hand*. That's what you call a cluster of bananas. Medium-sized. Three pounds?"

"Right on the money," TJ said, not sounding surprised. Storm did this all the time. "Here you go. Have a nice day!"

Gracie smiled to herself. She'd come to enjoy Storm's food facts. The chattering helped keep her mind from obsessing about the answering machine back at the cottage.

"That girl is really something," Eileen commented. Eileen Himmelberg — "Queen of the Supermarkets," as she was called on Gracie's blog — was head cashier at Big Lake Foods. She'd trained Gracie and kept her as her personal bagger ever since, even though Gracie suspected Eileen would have loved being Storm's cashier. Who wouldn't? Storm kept up her food-fact dialogues all day. The only drawback was that customers gravitated to Storm's lane, making it the busiest in the store.

"Do you think these bananas are too green?" a man was asking Storm.

Gracie glanced back to get a good look at him. She pegged him for about fifty, weighing close to 300 pounds. Not your average banana eater.

"No way!" Storm exclaimed. "Bananas are just about the only fruit that ripens best *off* the plant! At home, the starch will turn to sugar. So the riper it gets, the sweeter it will taste!"

As the day wore on, Gracie kept to herself. When they took their break, Storm asked her if something was wrong. Gracie considered telling Storm about Victoria and Thanksgiving and the answering machine. But what good would that do?

The afternoon dragged on. Gracie missed a lot of Storm's banana routine, but she learned more than she'd ever wanted to know about turkeys. Like the fact that the Apaches thought the turkey was too timid, so they wouldn't eat it or use its feathers on their arrows. Or that the toms — the male turkeys — gobble, but the hens click. About snoods and wattles and the wonders of all things turkey.

As soon as her shift ended, Gracie waved to Storm, then ran all the way to the cottage, slipping on the wet snow at every turn.

The only light inside the cottage was the blinking red of the answering machine. Without taking off her coat, Gracie dashed to the desk and punched the playback. She listened to the *whirr* of the rewinding tape.

"Hello. This is Ed Weese. We're the biggest real estate company in your neighborhood, and I'd like to —"

Gracie poked the answering machine, hoping, praying, that there was another message.

"Congratulations! Your number has been selected at random. You've been picked to spend a sunny three days and two nights in a Florida resort, where all of your golfing needs will be —"

Her hand trembled as she punched the "pass" button on the answering machine. She didn't hit it squarely and had to do it again. The tape whirred as it passed through the second message. Gracie's breath caught in her throat as she listened for the click of the off button. Or for another chance.

"Grace darling? Are you there?"

8

"—so you MUST call me, Grace! That's my private number. I'll be waiting."

The answering machine clicked off, and Gracie stood staring at it. She'd missed most of the message. The shock of hearing her mother's voice had done something to her ears. Victoria *had* called. And she didn't sound angry.

Gracie rewound the tape and played it again. She settled into the desk chair and listened as her mother's refined, musical voice filled the cottage. Closing her eyes, Gracie pictured Victoria, elegant in a white, sequined evening gown, her coal-black hair piled on top of her head, making a silky, cascading waterfall.

Gracie listened. And this time she heard the apology:

"Darling, I am so sorry! I cannot believe I forgot to call you when I said I would. Please forgive me? Things are so crazy here. People are so crazy. But you come first, Grace. Call me at this private number the minute you get this message! Promise?"

Gracie had to listen to the message a third time to take down the private phone number Victoria had given her. She hadn't known Victoria had a private number. Maybe it was

59

just for the job she was on. Was she still in Paris? She hadn't said. And what job was she on? Gracie had a million questions. But the most important one was whether her mother could come home for Thanksgiving.

Before she lost her nerve, Gracie dialed the number. The phone was picked up by automatic voice mail: "The party you're calling is unavailable. Please leave your name and number."

When it beeped, Gracie hung up. She'd had enough of leaving messages. This time, she wanted to talk to her mother. She tried again every five minutes for the next half hour, hanging up before the voice mail kicked in.

Cell phone in hand, Gracie headed back home. Her stomach growled, but she didn't think she'd be able to eat a thing. Not until she talked to Victoria. Her brain replayed the message, especially the part where her mom had said, "But you come first, Grace." Gracie wished she could have seen her mother's body language when she'd said that. This was the major reason Gracie hated the telephone. It hid all the important clues behind people's words.

Halfway home, the snow, or sleet, stopped. But the wind kicked up harder than ever. Turning her back to the wind and sheltering her cell behind a barren maple tree, Gracie hit "Send" twice to redial the private number.

This time it rang three times. "Yes?"

"Victoria? It's me. Grace. I—"

"Oh honey, I'm so glad you called." Away from the phone, she said, "Yes, yes! I'm coming." Back into the receiver, Victoria cleared her throat. "Grace, I'm on the air in fifteen seconds, sweetheart. It's a live interview."

Gracie could hear music and voices in the background. But she couldn't let her mother go. Not without asking her. Not after all of this waiting. "I want you to come here for Thanksgiving!" she blurted.

Silence.

"Did you hear me?" Gracie demanded. "I want to celebrate our birthdays like we used to."

"Sweetheart, they're calling me —"

"Will you come? Don't hang up! I need you to come." Gracie hated how desperate her voice sounded. Was she? Desperate?

"I — yes. Yes, sweetheart. Of course, I'll come. Call me later." The phone clicked.

"Victoria?"

There was nothing but the silent *shush* of the phone against her ear and the wild crackling of the wind through the stiff branches of the maple tree.

But Victoria Evers, formerly Doe, had said yes. Yes, she'd come for Thanksgiving. Yes, they could celebrate their birthdays like they used to.

Her mother was coming for Thanksgiving.

Gracie threw her cell into the air, then panicked as it came down into her open hands. *Thank you, God,* she prayed, her face lifted to the tiny white specks of snow that had begun to fall again. *Thank you!* Gracie knew it was the most sincere prayer she'd managed all week. She'd been guarding herself against a turn down from Victoria, holding back from hope. From prayer. Now her heart opened, and she could sense God with her under the branches and stars. He was smiling, telling

her how silly it had been for her to think she could hide anything from him.

*You knew how much I wanted her here. I know you knew. So,
thanks. Thanks for this.*

Gracie couldn't wait to tell Mick. She hit speed dial to ring
Mick's cell and started walking home again.

Mick answered right away. Gracie could tell she was still at
Sam's Sammich Shop. But it didn't stop Mick from letting out
an ear-splitting scream when Gracie told her the good news.

"Sweet!" Mick exclaimed, when she'd finished squealing.
"That is so like God, isn't it?"

"Yep." Gracie was grateful Mick couldn't see her right now,
blinking back tears. It was proving to be one of the rare times
she couldn't quite keep the cap on her bottle of emotions.
Maybe there were a couple of advantages to the telephone,
after all.

"Gracie, this will be the best Thanksgiving! Have you told
Mom yet?"

"That's where I'm headed right now." As she said it, she
reached the back door of the Doe household. She stepped inside
and kicked off her wet shoes. "I'm home, Munch. Better go."

"No, wait! Gracie, did I tell you how psyched I am for you?"

"Kind of figured, Munch," Gracie said, wriggling free of
her coat. "You know how perceptive I am." She paused, not
sure how to say what she was feeling. "Thanks, Mick." Then
she flipped the phone shut.

Lisa's reaction was almost as over the top as Mick's had
been. "Don't worry. I'll break the good news to your dad.
How long is Victoria staying?"

\

Gracie hadn't had time to ask. "A few days, I think." Long enough for Thanksgiving and birthday celebrations.

Birthdays! That meant ordering a cake, getting a gift. And not just any gift. What on earth could she get her mother that she didn't already have?

Up in her room, Gracie took out her notes from her interview with Murphy, the wide receiver. She read over what she had and wasn't that impressed with herself. The background was pretty complete. She'd included a play-by-play of the game he claimed was his favorite. She'd gotten a couple of good quotes. Still, it didn't read like a front-page feature.

Gracie felt her cell vibrate, then heard the chime. Her first thought was that Victoria was calling back. She flipped her cell and saw Annie's number. "Hey, Annie."

"Gracie! Mick told us about your mom. That is so tight!"

In the background, Gracie heard Storm's voice. "Hey, man! This is so filled with grooviness! Massively cosmic! Got to meet this well-tabbed mum of yours and check out the Gracie gene pool."

Gracie laughed.

Jazz came on. "Gracie, do you think we can show her some of my art? I mean, if she gets really bored? I thought she just wrote about adolescence and stuff, but Annie said she's an art critic too."

"Absolutely," Gracie answered. "A critic of many things." It was true. Victoria had become one of those people the news media dubbed "an expert." They'd have her on one show to talk about the aftermath of hurricanes, then invite her back to report on the funding of the arts in New York or Atlanta.

Annie got back on the phone. "Mom says it's Mick a la Mode on the house if you come back over here to celebrate."

"Wish I could," Gracie said, and she meant it. "I'm slammed. I've got that English outline due Monday. Plus, I have to turn in something on this big art project Jazz reminded me about. And I've got to finish up the article on Murphy for the paper. Thank your mom for me anyway, Annie. Pick up my rain check, okay?"

When she hung up, Gracie thanked God again, this time for her friends. Jazz and Storm hadn't even met Victoria yet. It felt good to know that the whole blog team was celebrating because they were happy for her.

Again, Gracie turned her attention to her article on John Murphy. She toyed with the headline: *Murphy the Magnificent, Mighty Murphy, Murphy on the Receiving End*. With every headline, she printed her byline. *That* part never changed: *by Grace Doe*. Gracie loved the way her name looked under the headlines. Simple. Strong. Straightforward. A name you could trust. She imagined Victoria catching a glimpse of the school paper spread out carelessly on Gracie's desk. Victoria's gaze would fall on the byline. Gracie's byline. She'd pick up the school paper, read that front-page article, and —

And what?

Gracie stopped daydreaming. Victoria Evers was a critic by profession. An author herself and a commentator on just about everything. If Gracie wanted to impress her mother, she had a lot of work to do.

9

Monday morning Gracie left another message for Victoria, asking when she'd be getting in for Thanksgiving. Then she hurried to school so she could hand in her feature in person.

Nobody was in the *Shark* newspaper office when she got there, so she camped outside the door to wait for Mr. Maxwell, the *Shark* advisor. To pass the time, she pulled out her notebook and observed a couple of students waiting to get into a classroom across the hall.

. . . .
THAT'S WHAT YOU THINK!
by Jane
NOVEMBER 23
SUBJECT: WAITING COMES IN FLAVORS.

There are as many different kinds of waiting as there are flavors of ice cream. But the biggest categories are hope and dread. All you have to do is observe the signs to see which group someone falls into.

Two students pace outside the same empty classroom in the halls of Typical High. The girl hangs on the doorknob, twisting her body slightly left, then right. Her eyes are wide as she presses her nose to the dark window. She glances away from the classroom and shoots a look down the hall as she rises on ballerina toes, then returns to earth. Translation: I'm waiting for something good.

The boy, on the other hand, paces. He stares at the floor in front of him. His predominant gesture is a neck crack, performed by jerking his head to the side. Twice, he shakes his head no for no apparent reason, other than in response to the voices in his head. Translation: I'm waiting for something bad.

My conclusion is that they are both waiting on the grade they so richly deserve.

Minutes later their teacher arrives, and my theory is confirmed. "Nice going on that test," Teach says to Eager Girl, who follows him in. After one more neck pop, the guy bravely shuffles in after them, no doubt to receive his bad grade.

"So what?" you ask. Well, shame on you. Haven't you ever been waiting on something? Something horrible or something wonderful? Do you want the whole world to know how uptight you are about it? Do you want to betray your feelings by your gestures when you're waiting on something? I know I don't.

Mr. Maxwell came shuffling up the hall. Gracie stopped writing and scrambled to her feet. She tucked away her notebook and got out her article.

Mr. Maxwell looked like he hadn't slept. Ever. Raccoon circles blackened his eyes. He always looked this way, but Gracie thought the look worked for him.

"Hey, Mr. Maxwell."

"Grace," he mumbled, as he fumbled with his briefcase. He patted all four pockets of his gray wool coat before coming

out with a key to unlock the *Shark* office. Stepping in ahead
of Gracie, he felt around for the light switch, found it, then
dumped his briefcase onto the desk. Or rather, onto the pile
of papers on the desk. Gracie figured it would have taken the
rest of the school year to get down to the actual desk. There
were bets going around the *Shark* office as to the color of
"Max's" desktop.

She held out her article. "This is the piece on Murphy, that
wide receiver you wanted me to write about."

"Fine." He kept rifling through papers on his desk.

She cleared her throat. But apparently, he didn't get the
hint. Pretty dense for a newspaper guy, Gracie thought.
"Mr. Maxwell, would you mind looking over the Murphy
piece now? I'm hoping it's good to go for page one, like you
planned. But if you can read it now, I could still have time to
add anything else you want in there."

He plopped into his desk chair, after brushing to the floor
a used Kleenex, a broken straw, and a host of unidentified
crumbs. With a singular motion, he snatched the pages out of
her hands and adjusted his reading glasses.

Gracie tried to look away while he read, but she couldn't
stop glancing at him. She searched his gestures and expres-
sion for signs of whether he liked the piece or not. His face
could have been wet cardboard as he flipped over page one
with a *snap*.

It was the closest thing to torture Gracie had experienced
in this office. She didn't mind rewrites. Every reporter had
rewrites. But this article wasn't like the others she'd written.
This one needed to be on page one. Gracie wanted Victoria to
see it.

Maxwell finally looked up. He flipped the pages back over and dropped the piece onto his desk. "Grace, you've done some good research here."

"I needed to." She was trying to be casual about it, but sweat trickled down her shirt. "I don't know much about football." Quickly, she added, "But I learned. I used the library. I talked to the coaches. Well, you know that." She pointed to the article.

"I'm not sure what to tell you," he began.

Something tried to rise in Gracie's throat, and she swallowed hard to get it back down. "Go on." His face was no longer unreadable. She almost wished it were. Maxwell hated the article. That much was clear. He was disappointed in it. In her.

"For page one, we have to give the reader something he didn't have before he read the article. Not just facts. We want to give him Murphy. Our readers need to walk away feeling like they know this kid, this John Murphy, wide receiver. Know him better than they did when they sat down to read the piece. I'm not getting that, Grace. You did a lot of things right here. Your facts are good. Thorough. But I'm not getting a picture of who Murphy is."

Gracie didn't know what to say. She wanted to promise him that she would fix the article. Not to worry. But she couldn't. How could she let the reader know Murphy. *She* didn't know him. She wasn't sure she knew how a person went about getting to know somebody either.

"I need heart!" Mr. Maxwell exclaimed, slamming one hand flat onto his desk. Papers scattered to the floor. "I need emotion! Grace, go back to John Murphy and let the readers in. Help them know this wide receiver. You've got until four o'clock tomorrow, or I'll have to run something else. Good luck."

It was all Gracie could do to stagger out of the *Shark* office. If Maxwell had told her anything else, if he'd wanted her to explain game strategy, college records, anything like that, she could have done the research. Grace Doe could research anything. Anything, maybe, except a human being. What Maxwell was asking her to do ran against everything in her life. He wanted heart. He wanted emotion.

Where was *she* going to get that?

The halls had filled. Students blurred together as Gracie made her way to class. *Father,* she prayed, *how am I going to do this? How am I going to rewrite with emotion? Or get to know John Murphy?*

Gracie slid through the crowd of students and realized she might as well have been swimming through a sea of strangers. How well did she know any of them? How on earth did anybody get to know anybody?

10

Gracie walked into art class a minute late, earning an evil-eye glare from their teacher, Ms. Biederman. Still dazed from the *Shark*-like brutal honesty of Editor Maxwell, Gracie eased to the back row, where a seat had been saved between Jazz and Storm.

"You okay?" Storm whispered. "I saw you in the *Shark* office. Guess you got your article in on time."

Ms. B. was glaring at them again. Gracie didn't want to get into it. Besides, it wasn't Storm's problem. "I got it in," she whispered. "Thanks."

"Bet you can't wait for your mom to come!" Storm said, not bothering to whisper. "I really want to meet her. Is she as filled with gorgeousness as she is in all those pictures at the cottage?"

Gracie had to think for a second. She'd seen the photographs so many times, they were like part of the wallpaper. Victoria accepting an entertainment award. Victoria shaking hands with her publisher. Victoria accepting the key to some city. Victoria on the cover of *Psychology Today*. "Yep. She looks just like that." *And I don't*, Gracie thought. It wasn't just

Gracie's short, blonde hair to Victoria's long, black hair. It was Victoria's elegance, the glamour that her daughter would never inherit.

Jazz leaned in. "Haven't you ever seen her mother on TV? Victoria Evers? Expert on ... whatever?"

"Your project outlines are due today, class," Ms. B. was saying. "Turn those in, and I'll look them over and hand them back before class ends. You can use the hour to work on your projects."

A low buzz took over the room as kids dug out their outlines and griped. Gracie wrote her name on the sheet she'd worked up the night before. It wasn't much.

Storm had a bag full of material scraps and pages of diagrams for a collage.

"Did you come up with an idea?" Jazz asked. Her own folder bulged with photographs, but she was just handing in a few pages of text. "What did you end up doing, Gracie?"

"I pulled together some of my nature blogs and tried to sketch a few pictures. Like illustrations." Gracie knew she'd never be an artist, but she could have done a better job on this project if she'd started earlier.

"Cool," Jazz said, glancing over at Gracie's pitiful drawings.

"That sounds majorly cool, Gracie!" Storm agreed. "Jazz said you hadn't started it yet. We were worried. But we should have known Grace Doe would pull it off."

Ms. B. walked by and collected their outlines. Gracie knew her project wasn't "majorly cool." She'd be lucky to get a C- out of it. And that was if she could get time to finish the illustrations. Her dad would freak when he saw her midterm grade in art.

After handing in her folder, Jazz leaned back in her chair, crossed her arms, and leveled an intense gaze at Gracie. "You're something, girl."

"What?" Gracie asked.

"Nothing shakes you. I'm freaking out about this project, so I've been working at it for weeks. I need an A to keep my parents off my back. And here you are, not even starting it until yesterday? And you're not worried at all."

"Chill, Jazz," Storm joked. "We can't all be Grace Does, you know."

Gracie elbowed them. She knew they were kidding. But she knew something else too. Her friends had no clue what it felt like to be Grace Doe.

Gracie went through the motions of school. But the wheels of her brain were trying to churn out a strategy for another Murphy interview. She didn't want to call on Annie again. And she was running out of time. Besides, getting the interview was only half the problem. A bigger problem was getting the emotion.

For the rest of the day, Gracie was determined to observe other people's emotions. Maybe that would give her some insight into how she was supposed to get "emotion" out of Murphy and into her article.

By the end of the day, she'd taken enough notes to fill several blogs. Her best observations had come from watching Annie Lind during lunch. Gracie's blog name for Annie was "Bouncy Perky Girl," the handle Gracie had used before getting to know Annie. She hadn't written about the "BP Girl" for a long time, and it was kind of fun to be back at it, although she planned to clear the blogs with Annie first this time.

THAT'S WHAT YOU THINK!
by Jane
NOVEMBER 23
SUBJECT: EMOTIONS ARE CONTAGIOUS?

It may or may not come as a surprise to you that I am not an emotional person. And yet, as a writer, I need to be able to capture emotion. I have to make my readers feel. Care. Know. And so today, I went in search of emotions in Typical High. I didn't have to go far.

At lunch, three girls quietly focused on their salads, ripping open tiny packets of dressing. Then Bouncy Perky Girl sat at the table. She was so perky that all three girls began chatting and giggling. Two more came, and the table could have bounced out of the cafeteria.

Then a strange thing happened. Rail-thin Girl sat down. Usually, this girl rivals the bounciness of our own BP Girl. But not today. Long face, slouched shoulders. After a few minutes of Rail-thin picking at her salad and staring at her fork, the others grew quiet. They stopped bouncing. A few words were exchanged. Bouncy Perky Girl didn't finish her salad. And when they walked away, they were all shuffling. No one was bouncing.

Something had happened to all of them. They caught Rail-thin Girl's emotion! I had witnessed an outbreak of epidemic sadness.

Question to ponder: Could emotions be catching?

Gracie's blog from her last class included an observation about Storm and Annie. Gracie still used "New Girl" as Storm's handle, but she hadn't written about her for quite a while either. Bringing up "New Girl" and "Bouncy Perky Girl" felt like old times.

THAT'S WHAT YOU THINK!
By Jane
NOVEMBER 23
SUBJECT: EMOTIONS SPREAD IN A CLASSROOM

I observed "Sleep-Deprived" snore his way through English and study hall today, and I admit I looked forward to seeing if the guy could get Bones, our history teacher, to explode in a fury of emotion. (Okay. I didn't claim this was a noble endeavor.)

But something entirely different came over the class. First, as expected, half of us "caught" Sleep-Deprived's yawn. Even I couldn't help yawning as I observed him.

Then New Girl changed things. "Enough!" she cried.

Sleep-Deprived stopped mid-snore, nearly choking himself.

New Girl turned to him. "Giraffes only sleep two hours a day. Eight should be plenty for all of us! Do you want to sleep away more than 122 days a year? I don't!"

There were murmurs of approval throughout the class, led by our own Bouncy Perky Girl. "She's right!" BP exclaimed. "I stayed awake for thirty-one hours once."

"Not bad. But think of Robert McDonald!" New Girl replied. "He holds the record for staying awake. Four hundred fifty-three hours and forty minutes."

New Girl entertained us for a few minutes with stats on dreams (that we average five a night or 1,825 a year). And how much of our awake time is spent blinking (fifteen times a minute, or 14,400 blinks a day).

By the time Bones finally took back the reins of the class, we were all wide awake. We'd caught New Girl's enthusiasm and let it replace Sleep-Deprived's boredom. Interesting to note that the first to catch the emotion, as usual, was Bouncy Perky Girl.

When class was over, Gracie stayed put until the room emptied. She needed to think. She'd observed emotions all day. And still, she wasn't sure she understood anything. How could she be so great at observing, but so rotten at understanding? She could read people's emotions from a distance, but she couldn't get inside.

Annie, on the other hand, might not even notice the gestures and expressions Gracie could read on people. Yet Annie was always there, in the middle of the emotion.

Suddenly, Gracie got an idea. Why hadn't she thought of it before? Who knew more about getting to the emotion, to the heart...

... than Professor Love?

11

At the cottage Gracie checked the answering machine to see if Victoria had left a message, but there was no blinking red light. Gracie still didn't know when her mother would arrive in Big Lake. All she knew was that when Victoria walked into the cottage, the first thing Gracie wanted her to see was the front-page story with Gracie's byline.

She sat at the computer and started searching the archives. Mick had created separate folders for outdated or unused blogs, along with a subfolder for Professor Love's e-mails. Sometimes Annie wrote back and forth with a reader, and none of the e-mails were ever posted on *That's What You Think!* Annie just kept the exchanges going so she could help the reader. She was always careful to tell them she was just a kid, like them, and that she had no training. But some of her advice was pretty amazing. Gracie thought that if she could study Annie's technique, the way she got people to open up, then maybe she could learn how to get emotion from Murphy.

THAT'S WHAT YOU THINK!

PROFESSOR LOVE

Dear Professor Love,

Everybody's baggin' on me, just because I like to date older guys. How can I convince them it's none of their business?

—Good4Me

Dear Good4Me,

How much older are we talking about here?

—Love, Professor Love

Dear Prof Love,

Not that it matters, but Evan is 27. I'm 16. Big deal.

—Good4Me

Dear Good4Me,

I'm 16 too. Eleven years may not be a lot when you're both old anyway, like 35 and 46. But it's a bigger deal at our age, don't you think? When he was 16, you were 5.

—Love, Professor Love

Prof Love,

So? The guy I liked last year was 29.

— Good4Me

Dear Good4Me,

Do your parents know?

— Love, Professor Love

Prof Love,

It's just my mom and me. And, no. She couldn't handle it. She wigged out on me last year when I told her I liked the 29-year-old.

— Good4Me

Dear Good4Me,

You're not going to like my advice. I know this because I wouldn't like it. But you need to tell your mom. Don't have secrets like this from her. It's not a safe world out there. She needs to know who you're dating.

— Love, Professor Love

Prof Love,

Oh great! Now you sound like her. You just don't get it. You don't know me or how I feel.

— Good4Me

Dear Good4Me,

I hear you. But I may get this more than you realize. I live with my mom too. My dad died in a plane crash when I was 2 months old. But it's funny. I still miss him. I didn't even know him, but I miss him.

— Love, Professor Love

Prof Love,

Mine didn't die. He took off on us when I was about five. Mom and I don't talk about him. But I guess I miss him. It's crazy, though. He was never around, even when he was still married to my mom.

— Good4Me

Dear Good4Me,

I know what you mean. It's almost like we miss the "office" of dad, don't you think? Sometimes, at the end of a rotten day, I'd just like to have a dad to come home to. I mean, I love my mom. But it would be cool to have a father who told me I was doing okay.

— Love, Professor Love

Prof Love,

Yeah.

— Good4Me

Dear Good4Me,

I admit that I'm boy crazy. Always have been. I've wondered if not having a dad around has made me more that way. Do you think missing your dad makes you want to be around older guys?

— Love, Professor Love

Professor Love,

Never thought about it. I don't know. Maybe.

— Good4Me

The exchange of e-mails went on for three days, getting more and more emotional. Gracie read and reread the e-mails until she felt she was onto something. It was when Annie opened up and talked about her father and her own problem with guys that Good4Me responded and revealed something more about herself.

Gracie moved on through the archives. Most of the e-mails, she remembered. But there was one Gracie didn't think she'd ever seen. Annie had shared with a reader about Sean, the guy Annie had thought she was in love with.

. . . .
THAT'S WHAT YOU THINK!

PROFESSOR LOVE

Dear Professor Love,

I'm dating the most amazing guy. Think of the hottest guy you've ever known and multiply by 10. So I don't really have a problem, right? It's just . . . well . . . sometimes he's not as nice as I'd like him 2 B. Or maybe it's that we don't always like the same things. He likes to party. I like him. He likes to hang with his buddies, who like to party. I like him. On the other hand, I like him and he likes him. My friends don't think he treats me right and I should break up with him.

But did I mention that he's so hot that people stop talking when he walks into the room?!

— Hopelessly-in-love

Dear Hopelessly-in-love,

Your guy sounds yummy. But maybe you should listen to your friends. And to yourself. Sounds to me like you're seeing some things on the inside that don't match how great he looks on the outside. I've been there. I had a homecoming date with a guy who was so hot he was blazing. Had myself convinced that I was in love. But my friends knew better. And they were right. He wasn't all that good-looking on the inside, where it counts. Not an easy lesson. I ended up dateless for homecoming (for the first and ONLY time, I assure you!). But I don't regret breaking up with him. That little voice you hear, telling you this guy isn't so nice on the inside, listen to it. Sometimes God whispers.

— Love, Professor Love

The door to the cottage opened, and Storm and Mick rushed in.

"It's freezing out there!" Storm exclaimed. She unzipped her leopard jacket and rubbed her hands together. Snowflakes floated from her sleek, black hair, as if she carried her own snowstorm.

Mick had exchanged her Indians ball cap for a blue stocking cap with the Indians logo. She shook it when she pulled it off. "What are you doing, Gracie? Studying?"

"Kind of."

Storm came around to the screen side. "Why are you reading Annie's old mail?"

"That's what I'm studying." Gracie leaned back in the chair. "I've got to re-interview Murphy and get some emotion into the story."

Mick, in stocking feet, joined them. "Annie's columns are loaded with emotion. Good idea, Gracie."

"Wait a minute," Storm said. "You already turned in your article, right?"

"Maxwell gave it back. He wants me to go deeper. Heart. Emotion. Stuff like that. I've got to let the reader get to know John Murphy." Gracie sighed. "So I thought I'd see how Annie does it. How she can get people to open up like she does."

"Did it help?" Mick asked. "Did you figure it out?"

Gracie tried to put her thoughts in a row. "I'm not sure. At first, I thought it was like an epidemic, or a plague. You know, like one person is sad and infects everybody else with sadness."

"Nice," Storm commented, her sarcasm showing.

"Hang on," Gracie pleaded. "But reading Professor Love's file ... well, I can see it's more like a give-and-take deal. Like

Annie tells them something about herself, and then the reader does the same thing."

"Yeah," Mick agreed. She hiked up her red wool socks. "Annie's not afraid to be vulnerable with people. I love that about her. I feel like I could tell Annie anything and she'd understand. She could identify, no matter how different we are. And we *are* different! She doesn't even like baseball. But it's like Annie gives you a piece of herself. And it makes you want to give a piece of yourself back to her."

"Sweet." Storm flopped onto the couch. "I never thought of it like that, but you're right. Annie's always right in there with you."

That's what Gracie had been picking up in the e-mails too. And in her friendship with Annie. In the past month, Annie had confided all kinds of things to Gracie. Only Gracie hadn't confided back.

"Okay," Gracie began, thinking out loud. "You're saying that if I want Murphy to open up, I've got to ... to what?" She still didn't get it. "Spill my guts? I can't do that."

"Just be honest with him," Storm offered. "Maybe he'll be honest back. Share a problem maybe. On second thought, that wouldn't work for you."

"Why not?" Gracie asked.

"Grace Doe doesn't have problems."

Gracie didn't have an answer to that. Was that really what Storm thought? That she didn't have problems? It was true that she almost never talked about them, but she sure had her share. She just didn't bother other people with her troubles. She didn't think they'd be interested.

No. That wasn't true. Gracie knew that her friends *would* have been interested in her problems. She had to admit that

she would have felt safe giving "pieces" of herself, her problems, to her friends. But still, she chose to keep those pieces
inside. She didn't even share most of them with God. It was
easier to wall them up and not make such a big deal out of
every problem that came along.

Mick jumped in. "Well, we know Gracie has one problem
at least. She needs another interview with John Murphy."

"So call him!" Storm cried. "Do you have his number?"

Gracie was grateful for Mick's rescue. "Yeah, I've got
his cell." It was one of the first things they'd taught her on
Shark staff. Get a number in case you have to double-check
information.

"Call him! Get that interview if you have to cry like a
baby!" Storm demanded. She popped up off the couch and
took Mick by the arm. "We'll even get out of your way. We
can hide in the bedroom."

"And pray!" Mick shouted, as she was dragged down the
hall.

Murphy answered on the fourth ring, and Gracie heard a
TV blaring in the background. She had to tell Murphy twice
who she was. "I won't take much of your time, Murphy. We
could meet at Sam's again. Or I could come to your house if
you want."

"I'm pretty busy tonight."

Right. "How about tomorrow before school then? I really
need this. Besides, wouldn't a front-page article make your
parents jazzed? Your number-one fans?"

She could hear his sigh over the phone. Then he said, "I
guess. I get to school early anyway."

"Thanks, Murphy," she said. "I'll wait in the gym, on the bleachers. Come as early as you can. I'll be there."

Mick and Storm burst from the bedroom as soon as Gracie got off the line with Murphy.

"You did it!" Mick exclaimed. "I guess we kind of eavesdropped."

"You rock, Ace!" Storm patted Gracie on the back.

"It's not over yet," Gracie cautioned. She was figuring it all out in her head. "Even if I get what I need from Murphy, I still have to rewrite the article and get it back to Maxwell before four o'clock tomorrow." That was the paper's absolute deadline for Wednesday's edition of the *Shark*.

"No problem!" Storm assured her.

Gracie forced a smile, although she didn't feel so sure. "No problem."

12

At home, Gracie worked up new questions for her Murphy interview. She tried to call Victoria again and left another message.

By the time Gracie got to homework, she had trouble keeping her eyes open. She kept nodding off over her art project. Not a good sign. Once, she actually had a minidream. She was juggling balls from her backpack. She kept reaching into her bag and pulling out another ball until she had dozens swirling over her head. In her dream she danced around frantically trying to keep them all in the air. She woke up when her stack of books crashed to the floor.

Gracie felt like she'd just climbed into bed when she heard someone calling her name.

"Gracie? Honey, wake up."

She rolled over and saw the tiny, shadowy form of Lisa, her stepmother. Gracie's first thought was *fire*! She flung back the covers and had one foot on the floor, when Lisa stopped her.

"Gracie, it's okay. Nothing's wrong. Your mother's on the phone." Lisa turned on the bedside lamp and held out the phone. Covering the mouthpiece, she whispered, "I think Victoria forgot about the time difference. She sounds fine. Don't worry."

Gracie sat on the edge of the bed while her heart took the beat down to normal. "Thanks, Lisa," she whispered, taking the phone. "Sorry about — "

"Don't be silly!" Lisa whispered. "I'm glad she called. Tell her we're looking forward to her visit." She tiptoed out of the room, her flannel nightgown sweeping the floor behind her.

Gracie took a deep breath and held the phone to her ear. "Victoria? Everything okay?"

Victoria sounded surprised at the question. "Okay? Yes! Of course. Why wouldn't everything be okay? How are *you*, honey? Is it as chilly there as it is in London?"

"London? I thought you were in Paris."

"No! I finished that boring assignment. And you'll never guess where Billy got me an entrée!"

Billy was her booking agent. Gracie had never met the man, but she admired him for working for Victoria all this time and never getting fired.

Before Gracie could guess where Billy had gotten Victoria "an entrée," Victoria answered her own question. "Buckingham Palace! I kid you not! *The* Buckingham Palace. Can you imagine? An American Thanksgiving dinner at Buckingham Palace? I won't be the only American media contact there, of course. It's clearly a PR move to get good press in America. But they're only inviting six of us, and I'm the only independent."

Gracie could feel her skin turning hard, trying to repel the words, to keep them from sinking in. "When? I mean, when are you supposed to be there?"

"For the dinner?" Victoria stopped. Gracie could picture her mother. She'd slap the heel of her hand to her forehead.

Not too hard. Her head would droop. Then came the sigh. "Oh, Grace. Don't hate me. I'll come to Ohio soon. I promise. I never should have agreed to Thanksgiving. Not before checking with Billy."

"That's okay." The words came automatically; that's how often Gracie had said them.

"I know!" Victoria sounded re-energized. "Let's do Christmas like it's never been done before! If you still want me to come to Big Lake, I'll do it. We can get Enrique to decorate the cottage. Wouldn't that be fun? And then, let's take off! Somewhere exotic! Anywhere you want to go!"

"That would be great, Victoria."

"You name it! Rome! Oh ... Venice at Christmas? Marvelous! Or Athens? Or the Islands?"

"Sounds great."

Victoria mentioned more possibilities, but Gracie didn't catch them. "Tell Liza thanks for the invitation, and maybe we'll do it next year."

"Lisa," Gracie corrected. "Okay."

"I'll make this up to you, honey. I'm going to send you the best birthday present you've ever gotten. What would you like, sweetheart?"

"You don't have to — " Gracie began.

"Of course I do! I'm your mother!"

When they hung up, Gracie turned off the lamp, but stayed sitting up in bed. Wind rattled the windows, and snow pelted the panes. Gracie shivered, but she didn't pull up the covers.

There was a knock at her bedroom door. Then the door opened, and Lisa tiptoed in. "I can put the phone back if you're done."

Gracie glanced around for the receiver and was surprised to find it still in her hand. "Thanks."

Lisa crossed the room and took the phone. "Everything all right?"

"What? Oh. Yeah. Fine." She slid down so she was lying curled up on top of the covers. "Victoria can't make it for Thanksgiving. One less place to set." Gracie heard her own voice, light and normal, as if it came from someone else. Someone light. Someone normal.

"Gracie," Lisa began, "I'm so sorry."

"Don't be, Lisa. It's so not a big deal. Really." She yawned and rolled over, turning her back on Lisa. "Victoria said to tell you thanks just the same. She really appreciates the invitation. She's looking forward to seeing you at Christmas. We're thinking we might celebrate here and then take a few days somewhere exotic, like Rome or Greece."

"Well, that would be fun." Lisa didn't sound excited, though. "Gracie, are you sure you're — ?"

"Thanks, Lisa," Gracie said, cutting her off. "I've got to get to school early tomorrow. I better get some sleep."

Gracie woke up early, hoping to leave for school before anyone got up. Instead, Mick and Lisa were already having breakfast, and the twins had finished theirs and were tossing Cheerios for the sport of it.

"Hi, Gracie," Mick said. She and Lisa stared up with pained expressions, as if somebody had died.

Gracie poured herself a big glass of orange juice. "I'm walking to school today. Have to be there early to finish up that Murphy article."

No response.

Gracie took a seat at the kitchen table.

"Want one?" Mick asked, holding up a box of powdered donuts.

Gracie couldn't remember the last donut she'd seen in the house. She wasn't hungry, but she took one anyway so Mick wouldn't think she'd lost her appetite. "Thanks."

"Mom told me," Mick said.

"Told you — ?"

"About Victoria not coming for Thanksgiving," Mick finished.

"Hope it was all right to tell Mick," Lisa said. She got up from the table and took a handful of Cheerios over to David and Daniel. More ammunition.

"Sure." Gracie smiled evenly. She'd been afraid of this, that Mick and Lisa would be worried about her. It was the kind of thing that could ruin *their* Thanksgiving. "It's no big deal, guys. I didn't really think Victoria would be able to get away on such short notice. It's cool. Seriously." She took the last bite of her donut, wiped her mouth, and started to get up.

"Wait." Mick was twisting her ponytail, like she did when she was worried. Gracie hated making things worse for everybody. Mick had her own problems. Middle school could be pretty tough. "Gracie, if you want to talk about it ..."

Gracie didn't want to talk about it. She hadn't even talked to God about it. She didn't want to think about it, in fact. But already, she felt little broken pieces slipping inside her. She got to her feet and put on her coat and gloves. "Hey, more turkey for us, right? And pumpkin pie? Seriously, I've got to get to school and get that interview. See you later."

In spite of the four inches of snow that had fallen overnight, Gracie got to school forty-five minutes early. She had to wait fifteen minutes before the "powers that be" would let students into the halls. Murphy hadn't shown yet, so Gracie hurried to the gym to wait. She picked the northwest corner of the empty bleachers where she could see both doors.

Waiting gave her too much time to think. Even though she'd been wakened from a deep sleep the night before, Gracie could remember every word her mother had said. She'd been so psyched about Thanksgiving with the Queen of England. Who could blame her? Who could compete with that?

Gracie glanced at her watch, then dug out her pencil. She needed her focus for this interview. Maybe if she prayed about the interview. *Father, please have Murphy show up, first of all. And help me ask the right questions. Help me relate to him, identify with him, draw him out. You know I'm lousy at that. I need you to help me get to know him.* She stopped praying. The instant she did, her mind was back on Victoria.

"Hey!"

Gracie looked up and saw John Murphy strolling in, unwrapping his scarf from his neck. He was wearing his letter jacket and a navy stocking cap.

"Hey, Murphy!" Gracie called, motioning him over. "Thanks for coming."

He climbed up the six rows of bleachers, without using the stairs, and sat on the bench below Gracie, which made them about the same height. "Sorry I'm late. Dad dropped me off. Like I don't know how to drive in snow." He unzipped his jacket and pulled off his cap.

"Has it started snowing again?" Gracie asked, fumbling for her interview questions.

"Supposed to get three more inches." He glanced over his shoulder at the door, as if he were planning his escape. Then he turned back to Gracie. "So, what did you forget last time?"

Scanning her list of questions, Gracie couldn't focus on any of them. They all sounded stupid. How could she ask him what made him angry? What made him sad? Annie — Professor Love — got those kind of responses, but she never asked direct questions. "I ... I don't know," she admitted. What made her think she could do this? She couldn't relate to this football hero. She couldn't even relate to her own mother.

"So why did you ask me here?"

Why *had* she asked him here? "Because I wanted a front-page article." She looked at him then, maybe for the first time. When she continued, her voice sounded weak and breathy. "The *Shark* advisor, Mr. Maxwell, said I had to get emotion into the piece or he wouldn't run it."

"Emotion? What does that mean?"

Gracie let out one bitter laugh. "You are *so* asking the wrong person." She felt as if her insides were shattering, breaking into jagged pieces that tore at her chest.

"Are you okay?" He leaned in, squaring his shoulders toward her, eyes narrowed, eyebrows lowered. Gracie could read the signals. John Murphy was sincerely concerned. About her.

"I'm fine," she answered. But that's not how she felt. She needed to collect herself, to keep going with the interview. But it all seemed so futile. She didn't know anything about emotion or relationships. And even if she wrote a super article, a front-page masterpiece, so what? Her mother would never see it.

She made herself look at him. "I'm sorry, Murphy. I shouldn't have wasted your time. I'm supposed to identify with you. Get you to open up. But you and I, we're in totally different worlds." And it wasn't just Murphy. She was in a different world from everybody, even her own mother. She thought about Murphy's parents, the way they never missed a game. "Remember how you told me your parents were your biggest fans? How can I identify with that? I can't even imagine what that would feel like." She wanted to stop herself, but she was so tired. The words were spilling out without her permission. "This morning, I found out that my mother doesn't even care enough to come here for Thanksgiving, even though she promised me she'd be here. More important things came up. Again. Even if I pull off this article, she won't see it."

"What does she do? Your mother, I mean."

"You'll like this," Gracie answered. "She writes books—counseling books about adolescence and things. She gets interviewed all the time as an expert. And she interviews really famous people."

"Cool."

"I guess. For her. But sometimes I wish she would inter-view *me*. I don't think she even knows I write for the paper. I just wish she cared more about what I do."

They were quiet for a minute, and Gracie could feel her cheeks burning. How could she have said those things? And to Murphy of all people? Her plan had been to find some-thing she could share with him, some way to get him to iden-tify with her. This sure wasn't it. If she could have found her voice again, she would have taken back every single word.

Finally, Murphy broke the awkward silence. When he did, it was almost as if he were talking to himself. "It's funny. Maybe parents just can't get it right. I mean, like, your mom. She's not invested in what you're doing. And *my* parents are *too* invested. Way too invested. They care *too* much."

He *so* did not get it. "Murphy, how can they care too much about you?"

"Maybe it's not *me* they care too much about." He was talking so softly she had to strain to hear him. "Sometimes I think they look at me out of uniform and don't even know me. We never talk about anything except ball. Football is *their* life more than it's mine. I don't even enjoy playing anymore. If I ever quit football, I don't think my parents would have anything to live for. Sometimes I think my football career is the only thing holding them together. Holding *us* together. Not me — just the career."

"Murphy? What's up, man?" Two of Murphy's football buddies frowned from the door.

"Right there, guys!" Murphy stood up fast, knocking Gracie's unused pencil out of her hand. "You know how it is when you're famous, guys!" he shouted down to them. "Interview after interview." He turned back to Gracie, nodded quickly, then leaped to the floor to join his buddies.

Other students had trickled into the gym. Gracie hadn't noticed them before. She sat where she was and tried to replay what had just happened. Slowly, the realization crept in that somehow, miraculously, she had gotten to know John Murphy. She'd gotten emotion.

How had that happened? She replayed their conversation in her head, amazed that she'd told him so much about

Victoria. In spite of herself, she'd opened up to Murphy. And, just like in Professor Love's letters, Murphy had returned the favor. He had opened up to her.

She'd gotten exactly what she needed for her article. Now all she had to do was write.

13

Gracie had to skip lunch and opt out of study hall, but by the end of the day, she had her feature on John Murphy. She turned it into Kyle Baker, the student managing editor, who could be tougher on writers than Mr. Maxwell. But as she watched Kyle read the article, she knew she'd gotten it right.

"Now that's what I'm talking about," Kyle muttered. "Not bad at all."

Sticking around for the edits and helping out in the *Shark* office made her miss her ride home with her stepbrother, Luke. But Gracie didn't mind. She was basking in the knowledge that she was finally getting her front-page article. If Victoria wouldn't come to the article, then at least Gracie could send the article to Victoria.

Gracie felt so good pulling off the feature that it surprised her how fast all the good feelings dissolved in the cold dusk as she walked home. By the time she reached her house, she couldn't resurrect a single good feeling about the article. Vague doubts had begun to gnaw away at her. What would her mother think of the story? And Murphy? What would he think?

Gracie didn't want to think about Murphy. Her editor had asked her to get emotion, and she'd gotten it. Murphy would have to understand.

The rest of the night, Gracie holed up in her room and hammered out her art project, trying not to think of anything else. Mick must have told the blog team about Victoria's change of plans because they all called to check up on her. Gracie told them the same thing. She was fine. Victoria would come at Christmas instead. It was no big deal. She had a lot of homework.

On Wednesday morning after a rotten night's sleep, Gracie hitched a ride with Luke and Mick. With one foot already in Ohio State, Luke had started upping the volume on his complaints about high school. "Why would they make us go to class at all today? Nobody's going to get anything done. We should have taken off the whole week. At Ohio State, if you want to be absent, you just don't show. Nobody cares."

Gracie doubted that, but she didn't feel like arguing with her stepbrother. Luke could drive her postal, treating her like a little kid. But she was going to miss him next year.

"At least it's just a half day," Mick offered from the backseat.

"Yeah," Luke conceded. "Well, I'm out of here at noon on the nose. Be here, or walk home. Deal?" He glanced over at Gracie who was riding shotgun. "I hear my little sister snagged the front page of the *Shark* this week."

"Where'd you hear that?" Gracie asked, trying not to betray how excited she was about seeing her byline.

"Juliana maybe?" Luke answered, stopping behind a school bus that already looked overloaded. Two boys pressed their

faces against the back window, turning their noses into bug
splats. "Or Kristin? Can't remember for sure. Maybe it was
Marissa." Luke was so popular that he couldn't keep track
of his "friends who were girls." Not to be confused with his
"girlfriends."

"That's so tight, Gracie!" Mick exclaimed, leaning as far up
as her seatbelt allowed. "Can we get a bunch of copies? I want
one for me and one for Ty and one for Mom and Dad. You
should send one to Victoria!"

"Hmm. Maybe," Gracie answered, as if she hadn't already
thought of that ... a million times.

Luke pulled into a scooped-out parking spot in the senior
lot. Mick thanked him for the lift, then hopped out and ran
across the snowy yard to the middle school. Luke got side-
tracked by two blondes before he'd even turned off the engine.

Gracie glanced at the sky before walking up the sidewalk
alone. Gray, puffy clouds threatened, or promised, more snow.

"Nice article," Juliana said, as she passed Gracie in the
hall. "Can't believe you got all that stuff out of Murphy."

"Thanks," Gracie muttered. She should have felt great.
Proud. Juliana, who worked on the student paper, had never
once said anything positive about Gracie's pieces for the *Shark*.

But for some reason, Gracie couldn't shake the uneasi-
ness gnawing at her. Something was nagging at her inside.
She just didn't want to listen to anything deep inside because
everything was too messed up below her surface.

The *Shark* edition wasn't out yet, so Gracie went on to
class. Luke had been right about nobody getting any work
done. Even teachers seemed to be on some kind of mental
Thanksgiving vacation.

Between classes, Gracie checked the newspaper drop-offs. It wasn't until her last class ended that she saw students with this week's *Shark*. She ran to the office to get her copies.

Gracie picked up the newspaper, and there it was. Page one, above the fold: "Starring John Murphy" by Grace Doe.

Gracie told herself that Murphy had to love the headline. What guy wouldn't want to be considered a "star," right? She'd been silly to worry about it.

Grabbing her copy, she found a quiet spot by the gym, where she could lean against the wall and read the piece. The first part was solid research and reporting, mixed with quotes from Murphy and the coaches. But toward the middle, the article changed focus. Gracie had used most of her conversation with Murphy on Tuesday, leaving out her end of it, of course. She'd quoted him word for word on his parents and career. She could see why Kyle had liked the article better this way. There was more emotion, all right.

"Grace Doe! Stay where you are!" John Murphy stormed down the hallway toward the gym. His shoes squeaked as he barreled toward her. Behind him came what looked like half the football team. Murphy waved a crumpled copy of the *Shark*. "Thanks a lot for this!" His neck muscles were tightened into cords, and his jaw jutted out in front of him. "Why would you write lies about me?"

"Lies?" Gracie knew she hadn't made up things.

"Nobody's going to believe this trash!" he shouted. He glanced back at his teammates, who were sauntering up, as if afraid to get too close.

"Murphy, I'm sorry." She was too. Somewhere deep inside, she'd known this was how Murphy would react. But she'd

ignored her own doubts. Her own feelings. She hadn't wanted
to think about anything except having a front-page article to
show her mother.

Murphy threw up his hands. "What good does 'sorry' do
me when you've already lied about everything?"

"Murphy, I didn't lie. You said those things, and — "

"Yeah? Well, *you* said things too!" Murphy wheeled around
to the half dozen guys behind him. "You guys know Grace
Doe, ace reporter, don't you?"

Gracie couldn't breathe. She couldn't look at them, but she
couldn't look away.

"No? You don't know Grace Doe?" Murphy sounded surprised, but his body language spelled fury, not surprise. "I
guess you wouldn't know her. She doesn't date much. And
when she does, she tends to get stood up."

A couple of the guys laughed. Gracie started to protest.
She'd never been stood up. How could she? She'd never really
had a date.

"In fact," Murphy continued, "this year she's been stood up
for Thanksgiving."

Gracie felt sick to her stomach. She knew what was
coming.

"Sad but true," Murphy continued. "Poor Grace Doe got
stood up ... by her own mother. Ouch." He glared one last
time at Gracie, then joined his buddies. "Come on, man. Let's
get out of here. I need some fresh air."

Gracie's chest heaved as if everything building up inside of
her was about to explode into the universe.

"Gracie, there you are!"

She heard Annie's voice and squinted through blurry eyes to see Annie and Storm, both with copies of the *Shark*.

"Have you seen John yet? He's so upset!" Annie didn't sound angry. More like baffled.

"You'd better lie low, girlfriend," Storm advised. "That man is on a mission, and you're not going to want to be there when he lands."

"Gracie?" Annie put one hand on Gracie's shoulder. "What's going on? Talk to us."

Gracie shook her off. She couldn't talk to them. She couldn't even look at them. All she knew was that she had to get out of there before everything fell apart. Before the broken pieces inside of her came raining down on all of them.

14

Gracie took off running. On her way out the door, she stuffed her newspaper into the trash. When she turned back around, she bumped into somebody.

"Hey, man. What's — ?"

It was Jazz, but Gracie couldn't stop. She pushed past her, nearly sliding down the salted steps.

Snow came down hard, swirling across the road like slithering snakes. Gracie kept running, letting the pain in her side keep her mind from other pain. The pain in her mind. Her heart.

She didn't look up, didn't plan her route. But she ended up at the cottage. Panting, she unlocked the door and practically fell inside. It took her a minute to catch her breath. She hadn't worn gloves or a hat, and her fingers were pink. When she shook her head, water sprayed the white carpet.

On every wall, Victoria stared down at her. Gracie had never realized how many photographs there were of her mother here. Beautiful Victoria. Glamorous Victoria staring down at her plain-Jane daughter.

Gracie burst into tears. Her knees buckled, and she dropped to Victoria's white carpet.

The door opened behind her.

"Gracie! What are you doing on the floor?" Mick sounded frantic.

Behind Mick came Storm, Annie, and Jazz.

"Is she all right?" Annie whispered.

Jazz shut the door against the wind. "I knew this is where you'd come. What happened back there?"

They circled Gracie, sitting cross-legged, as if they were on a campout and Gracie were the fire. Gracie tried to sniff back tears. "I just wanted to do what you guys do all the time! What Annie does in her columns."

"Me?" Annie asked.

Gracie knew she wasn't making sense. "I opened up to Murphy, and he threw salt in my open wounds!" She thought about it. "Just like I did to his wounds when he opened up to me. See? I told you. I'm not like you. I don't know anything about emotions. Or relationships. Or sharing problems."

"With Murphy?" Jazz asked. "You shared your problems with *him*?"

Gracie nodded.

Storm filled Jazz and Annie in on Mr. Maxwell's assignment to get more emotion into Murphy's story and on Gracie's research into the "Professor Love" archives.

"So that's why Murphy told you that stuff?" Annie asked. "Well, that's good then, right? You shared something with him. You were vulnerable. And he opened up to you. That's good, Gracie. He gave you a piece of himself."

"Yeah," Storm agreed. "Only, he probably didn't expect to see his very private life plastered on the front page of the *Shark*."

Gracie knew Storm was right. "Well, he sure got even."

"What do you mean?" Mick asked.

"He told the whole team I'd been stood up for Thanksgiving by my own mother."

Nobody said anything for a minute. Then Mick threw her arms around Gracie. "Gracie, I'm sorry. We didn't mean you should share everything with him. You don't know him that well."

"I didn't mean to!" Gracie protested. "It was like I exploded all over him."

"You kept it inside too long," Mick said softly.

Gracie wanted to bolt. Things were getting way too personal. She could stuff all of this back inside, grin, and bear it.

Or could she? *Father, I don't want to bear it. It's too heavy.*

She swallowed hard, then looked up at her friends. "I really wanted my mother to come."

Mick hugged her again, and it felt good to have those little arms squeeze tight. "I know, Gracie. I knew you were counting on having her come."

"You did? *I* didn't," Storm said. "You acted like everything was fine, Gracie. You said it was no big deal."

Tears were filling Annie's big eyes. "And I bought it too. I'm sorry, Gracie. I didn't know you were going through this."

Jazz looked as uncomfortable as Gracie felt. "You're great at observing us. I guess we're not so hot at observing you."

Storm sprang up and paced the room. "Does Victoria know how upset you are? I hope she feels lousy for letting you down!"

"Victoria doesn't let herself feel lousy." The second she said it, Gracie realized she could have been talking about herself.

She'd done everything *not* to feel. She'd even tried to keep her prayers from going too deep, where it would hurt to feel.

Annie was all-out crying now. "I'm such a wing-nut airhead for believing you when you said everything was fine."

"It's not your fault. It's mine," Gracie admitted. "When Victoria told me she wasn't coming, I tried to convince myself I didn't really care. That was just Victoria. I mean, why should she come back for me? If I'd been elected homecoming queen or something — yeah — then maybe she'd come."

"Oh, Gracie," Mick said.

"That's whack!" Storm exclaimed.

Gracie appreciated their support. But she didn't want to stop now. "I guess I thought I could handle everything myself. I feel like I've been juggling, but suddenly I can't keep the balls in the air. They're way too heavy."

Storm reached over and brushed Gracie's hair off her forehead. Nobody spoke. Then Storm exclaimed, "The verse! Mick's verse! Did you see it, Gracie?"

Gracie remembered how she'd felt when she read Mick's verse about Jesus saying that the burden is light. "I read it, but my burden is so not light. I don't think that one's doing it for me, Storm."

"Not that verse! The new one. The one Mick put up today!" Storm turned to Mick. "Read it to her."

Mick fished out her Bible and opened to Galatians 6:2. " 'Carry each other's burdens, and in this way you will fulfill the law of Christ.' "

"Isn't that tight!" Storm cried. "Man, that's right on! You carry ours all the time, Gracie. But you've got to let us carry yours too."

Gracie drank in the verse. *"Carry each other's burdens." Is that how it worked?* Could she share her problems with her friends? Would that really make them lighter?

"And it goes with that other verse," Mick explained, "the one about Jesus' burden being light. He carries your problems if you let him, Gracie. And we get to help, if you let us."

It did make sense, Gracie thought. Maybe if she'd talked to God sooner and if she'd let her friends help, she wouldn't have been carrying around a pack full of lead balls that refused to be juggled.

For the next hour, Gracie talked. Whenever she stopped, one of her friends urged her to go on. So she did. They lit the gas fireplace and settled in around it, with Gracie in the middle. "Did you know I was a breech baby?"

"Is that when you're born backward?" Mick asked.

Storm grinned. "I hope you appreciate how many one-liners I'm holding in right now about being born backward."

"Same here," Jazz agreed.

Gracie laughed. Then she got serious again, and so did her friends. "I like to think that maybe I knew something even back in the womb. Like maybe they had to pull me out by my feet because I was hanging on to Victoria, knowing it would be the last time we'd ever be close."

She'd never told anybody that, not even God. Now, as she opened up, she could sense God's presence as much as if he were sitting cross-legged in front of the fire with them.

Annie fixed peanut butter sandwiches, and they moved to the kitchen where the afternoon sunlight was already fading.

"So how mad do you think John Murphy really is?" Gracie asked.

"On a scale of one to ten," Storm began, "I'd say a hundred and forty-seven."

They laughed.

"I don't know how I can make up for what I did. I'll call him and apologize," Gracie said.

"Good start," Annie agreed.

They stayed until it turned dark out and they had to go home. It was great to laugh again. Gracie wouldn't have believed it possible. She and Mick said goodbye to Jazz, Annie, and Storm and walked home. Gracie wondered if she could float. That's how light she felt with her problems unpacked. Shared. Moonlight broke into tiny silver and gold pieces that danced on the snow all around them. She'd given pieces of herself to her friends and more pieces to God. And what had she gotten back? A whole that was so light she felt she might float all the way to heaven.

Internet Safety by Michaela

People aren't always what they seem at first, like wolves in sheep's clothing. Chat rooms, blogs, and other places online can be fun ways to meet all kinds of people with all kinds of interests. But be aware and cautious. Here are some tips to help keep you safe while surfing the web, keeping a blog, chatting online, and writing e-mails.

- Never give out personal information such as your address, phone number, parents' work addresses or phone numbers, or the name and address of your school without your parents' or guardian's permission. It's okay to talk about your likes and dislikes, but keep private information just that—private.

- Before you agree to meet someone in person, first check with your parents or guardian to make sure it's okay. A safe way to meet for the first time is to bring a parent or guardian with you.

- You might be tempted to send a picture of yourself to new friends you've met online. Just in case your acquaintance is not who you think they are, check with your parent or guardian before you hit send.

- If you feel uncomfortable by angry, threatening, or other types of e-mails or posts addressed to you, tell your parent or guardian immediately.

- Before you promise to call a new friend on the telephone, talk to your parent or guardian first.

- Remember that just because you might read about something or someone online doesn't mean the information is true. Sometimes people say cruel or untruthful things just to be mean.

- If someone writes creepy posts, report him or her to the blog or website owner.

Following these tips will help keep you safe while you hang out online. If you're careful, you can learn a lot and meet tons of new people.

Subject: Michaela Jenkins

Age: 13 on May 19, 7th grade at Big Lake Middle School
Hair/Eyes: Dark brown hair/Brown eyes
Height: 5'

"Mick the Munch" is content and rooted in her relationship with Christ. She lives with her stepsis, Grace Doe, in the blended family of Gracie's dad and Mick's mom. She's a tomboy, an avid Cleveland Indians fan, and the only girl on her school's baseball team. A computer whiz, Mick keeps *That's What You Think!* up and running. She also helps out at Sam's Sammich Shop and manages to show her friends what deep faith looks like.

Subject: Grace Doe

Age: 15 on August 19, sophomore
Hair/Eyes: Blonde hair/Hazel eyes
Height: 5', 5"

Grace doesn't think she is cute at all. The word "average" was meant for her. She dresses in neutral colors and camouflage to blend in. Grace does not wear makeup. She prefers to observe life rather than participate in it. A bagger at a grocery store, only her close friends and family can get away with calling her "Gracie." She is part of a blended family and lives with her dad and stepmom, two stepsiblings, and two half brothers. Her mother's job frequently keeps her out of town.

Subject: Annie Lind

Age: 16 on October 1, sophomore
Hair/Eyes: Auburn hair/Blue eyes
Height: 5', 10"

Annie desperately wants guys to admire and like her. She is boy-crazy and thinks she always has to be in love. She considers herself to be an expert in matters of the heart. Annie takes being popular for granted because she has always been well-liked. She loves and admires her mom. Her dad was killed in a plane crash when Annie was two months old. Annie helps out at Sam's Sammich Shop, her mom's restaurant. She can be self-centered, though without being selfish.

Subject: Jasmine Fletcher

Age: 15 on July 13, freshman
Hair/Eyes: Black hair/Brown eyes
Height: 5', 6"

Jasmine is an artist who feels that no one, especially her art teacher and parents, understands her art. She is African American and has great fashion sense, without being trendy. Her parents are quite well-to-do, and they won't let Jasmine get a job. She has a younger brother and a sister who has Down syndrome. She also had a brother who was killed in a drive-by shooting in the old neighborhood when Jazz was one.

Subject: Storm Novello

Age: 14 on September 1, freshman
Hair/Eyes: Brown hair/Dark brown eyes
Height: 5', 2"

Storm doesn't realize how pretty she is. She wishes she had blonde hair. She is Mayan/mestiza, and claims to be a Mayan princess. Storm always needs to be the center of attention and doesn't let on how smart she is. She dresses in bright, flouncy clothing, and wears too much makeup. Storm is a completely different person around her parents. She changes into her clothes and puts her makeup on after leaving for school. Her parents are very loving, though they have little money.

Here's a sneak preview of the next book in the Faithgirlz! Blog On series, now available!

1

THAT'S WHAT YOU THINK!
PROFESSOR LOVE
MARCH 10

Dear Professor Love,

Life is SO not fair! My 2 sisters have boyfriends. They've always had boyfriends. And when they break up (They always do the breaking. Nobody ever breaks up with them!), they get new boyfriends within the week. They have dates every weekend. The only dates I have are pity dates, when my friends fix me up with their guy friends. I've suffered through so many blind dates, my sisters say I should get a guide dog.

What should I do?

—Boyfriendless

Dear Boyfriendless,

Take a deep breath, girlfriend! I know where you're coming from because I've been there. But I'm working on changing my tune. Why do we think we have 2 have boyfriends? Sounds like your sisters aren't doing so well in that department if they're breaking up all the time, right? Maybe you and those friends of yours should stop the blind date train and just go out together. Have fun! Develop friendships with guys. BTW, a date can be the worst place for friendships! And breakups can be the worst thing for friends.

But maybe your sisters are right about 1 thing. Get a dog — dogs rock!

Love, Professor Love

Annie Lind leaned back and admired her work as Professor Love. The whole *That's What You Think!* blog team had met at the cottage earlier, like they did most Saturday mornings. Annie had taken up half the time telling them her big news: her cousin Shawna would be coming to Big Lake for the summer. Annie didn't know if she could wait two whole months.

Since she still had an hour to kill before cheerleading practice, Annie hung around after the meeting was over. She adored the cottage, with its giant fireplace, wooden beams, and white stucco walls. It belonged to Gracie's bio mom, who was off in Europe someplace. The cottage was perfect for writing her love advice column.

She got back to it.

Dear Professor Love,

I'm in love with Jennifer. And I totally trust her. It's just that there are so many guys at my school who would

*like to have my Jennifer. And she's so friendly with
everybody. I get crazy when I see her talking with some
guy by her locker or in the cafeteria or after school. When
I can't find Jen, or I call her and she doesn't pick up, or
I drive by her house and see her car gone, I fly into a
jealous rage. I'm afraid my jealousy will drive her away.*

*Is it expecting too much for her to let me know where she
is at all times?*

— Watchdog

Annie didn't even have to think about this one. She set her
fingers to the keyboard.

Dear Watchdog,

*Hmm . . . Is it 2 much 2 expect for you 2 know where
Jennifer is at all times? Of course not — as long as she's in
prison. That's the only way you can be sure where she is
every minute.*

*Sounds like the problem isn't Jennifer. It's you, Watchdog!
You're jealous without cause. I suggest you get a grip.
Actually, I suggest you loosen that grip!*

Love, Professor Love

Dear Professor Love,

*Why is life so unfair? I'm a nice person. I'm not hot, but
i'm okay to look at. Still, my whole life it's seemed like
everybody is more popular than i am. When girls hit the*

mall, nobody thinks 2 ask me. I'm left out when they go 2 a game together or just hang out before school. I wish i could trade lives. It's always been like this. If there are three of us, i'm the odd girl out. Hey—when i was little, i had two imaginary friends. They wouldn't let me play with them.

—The unfair maiden

Annie laughed out loud at that one. Then she typed her answer:

Dear Maiden,

Don't trade places with anyone! Sounds to me as if you have a great sense of humor. (I LOL at your exclusive imaginary friends!)

Most people in middle school and high school feel like the odd person out. (It's one of the best kept secrets of high school!) Don't forget that you're exactly the person God wants you to be. You think God makes mistakes? No way! Without you, there would be a hole in the universe!

Love, Professor Love

Annie stopped typing and glanced through the rest of the e-mails in her "Professor Love" pile. There was a question — more like a gripe — from a kid who studied hard for B's, while his brother got A's without studying. Somebody who called herself Two-Ton began her e-mail with the same two words that kept popping up: *No fair!*

"Gracie!" Annie shouted. She *had* to see this. Annie scrolled down and found another e-mail complaining about life's unfairness. "Gracie! I think I've got our blog theme!"

That did it. Annie heard the squeak of chair legs on the wood floor, followed by Gracie's footsteps overhead.

"You better not be playing me, Prof," Gracie warned, bounding down the stairs two at a time. In seconds, she was reading over Annie's shoulder. "I'd just about given up on a theme."

When they'd ended the blog meeting, Gracie's instructions had been for everybody to write their columns, and she'd figure out a theme later. Several months ago Grace Doe had started the anonymous blog with the help of her little sister, Mick, the computer guru. Annie, Storm, and Jazz had been brought on board later. Gracie, the unofficial boss, could be officially bossy, especially about blog themes. But this time Annie felt sure she had the perfect theme.

"No fair!" Annie said. Gracie narrowed her green eyes at Annie. Annie thought Gracie's eyes were her best feature. That, and her relatively small feet. But then Annie noticed everybody's feet because they were all smaller than her own.

"You called me down here to complain?" Gracie inhaled, as if not choking her friend required superpowers. "I was in the middle of my blog, Annie! What's so unfair?"

"I'm not complaining. That's the theme — *No fair*!" Annie pointed to the screen, where her "Professor Love" column was still displayed. Gracie moved in closer. She shoved her short, straight blonde hair off her forehead and frowned as she read.

"Hmmm. Might work. I'm liking it." She moved the curser. "Cool. No fair. Should be easy to blog on that." Finally, she grinned at Annie. "Not bad."

"Aw, you don't have to gush, Gracie," Annie teased. Gracie's dimple showed, even though Annie could tell how hard she was trying to maintain her tough-guy blog editor persona.

The door flew open, and Gracie's little stepsis, Mick, rushed in. Sweat glistened on her forehead, even though all she wore were jeans and her Cleveland Indians T-shirt.

"Mick, where's your jacket?" Gracie called.

"Outside. With Ty. We're getting in some great batting practice. I just came back to get us something to drink. You should see Ty's swing! He's going to hit hard this spring." Mick kicked off her shoes and dashed through to the kitchen.

Annie knew Mick would have played ball all day and night if she could have. Mick felt about baseball the way Annie did about cheerleading. "Hey, Mick! Is it nice out?" March in Big Lake, Ohio, could bring spring in the morning and snow at noon.

"Annie?" Mick squinted into the room. She wasn't wearing her glasses. Probably because she'd broken three pairs so far this year playing ball. "I didn't even see you there. Sorry! Why aren't you at cheerleading practice?"

"It doesn't start 'til ten."

Mick frowned. "Are you sure? Ty and I were playing catch behind the gym. It sure sounded like cheerleading practice."

Annie glanced at the clock. 9:40. "That doesn't make any sense. Bridget told me last night that practice wouldn't start until — "

"Bridget?" Grace interrupted. "As in Bridget Crawford?" Annie nodded.

Gracie sighed. "Annie, how many times do I have to tell you, listen to that girl's body language, not her words? Didn't you tell me she's angling for your spot on the squad? The pyramid topper, or whatever you call it?"

"Flyer." Annie had been a flyer since the fall. By rights, the position shouldn't have gone to a sophomore. Or to anyone as tall as Annie. But she was fearless, lightweight, and peppy.

Ms. Whitney, their coach, said nobody smiled more than Annie on the court. Nobody had more expressions, which was a big part of flying during stunts. Still, Annie knew she'd have to fight to keep her position.

"I can't believe I let Bridget pull this on me!" She fumbled with her bag, stuffing everything back in. *"Annie's Rule: Never believe a rival!* Why don't I listen to myself?" She slipped one arm into her jacket.

Mick opened the door for her. "Maybe Bridget got the times mixed up."

"Right." Annie could have kicked herself for falling for it. This was vintage Bridget. "Later, guys! This is war!"

Annie raced to Big Lake High. The sun peeked in and out of moving clouds that covered most of the sky. The trees weren't fooled by the sunshine. The only leaves were brown hangers-on from fall.

Outside the gymnasium, Annie paused just long enough to catch her breath. Inside, the squeak of tennis shoes echoed off the walls, and Ms. Whitney's voice barked out orders: "Arms straight! Chin up! Eyes on the flyer!"

Eyes on the flyer?

But they didn't have the flyer. *Annie* was the flyer. Annie shoved open the gym door just in time to see the Big Lake Sharks cheerleaders finishing their new tumbling routine. And right in the center — just like they'd been practicing for competition — stood the mini-pyramid, Elevator. With Bridget on top.

faiThGirLz!
2 corinthians 4:18

Inner Beauty, Outward Faith

Grace Notes
Softcover • ISBN 0-310-71093-6

Busted! An anonymous teenage blogger comes in from the cold ... Grace Doe, an astute observer of human nature, prefers blogging about her high school classmates to befriending them—and she likes being a loner just fine, thanks.

Love Annie
Softcover • ISBN 0-310-71094-4

The Professor of Love needs to go back to class ... Annie Lind thinks she was born to be "Professor Love," her advice column identity in the newly expanded "That's What YOU Think" website. She knows how to handle guys!

Just Jazz
Softcover • ISBN 0-310-71095-2

Jazz is working on a masterpiece: herself ... Jasmine "Jazz" Fletcher is an artist down to her toes; she sees beauty and art where others see nothing. And her work on the website is drawing rave reviews. But if she doesn't come up with a commercially successful masterpiece pretty soon, her parents may make her drop what they consider an expensive hobby to focus on a real job.

Storm Rising
Softcover • ISBN 0-310-71096-0

Nobody knows the real Storm ... not even Storm! The center of attention wherever she goes, Storm Novelo is impetuous, daring, loud—and a phony. Convinced that no one would like her inner brainiac, she hides her genius behind her public airhead.

Available now at your local bookstore!

zonderkidz

faiThGirLz!
2 corinthians 4:18

Inner Beauty, Outward Faith

With TNIV text and Faithgirlz! sparkle, this Bible goes right to the heart of a girl's world and has a unique landscape format perfect for sharing.

The Faithgirlz! TNIV Bible • Hardcover • 0-310-71002-2

The Faithgirlz! TNIV Bible • Faux Fur • 0-310-71004-9

Available now at your local bookstore!

faiThGirLz!™
2 corinthians 4:18

Inner Beauty, Outward Faith

My Faithgirlz! Journal
0-310-71190-8

Faithgirlz! NIV Backpack Bible
Italian Duo-Tone™, Periwinkle
0-310-71012-X

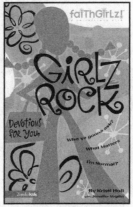

Girlz Rock:
Devotions for You
0-310-70899-0

No Boys Allowed:
Devotions for Girls
0-310-70718-8

Chick Chat:
More Devotions for Girls
0-310-71143-6

Available now at your local bookstore!

faiThGiRLz!
2 corinthians 4:18

Inner Beauty, Outward Faith

Now available from **inspirio**

Faithgirlz! Bible Cover
Large ISBN 0-310-80780-8
Medium ISBN 0-310-80781-6

Faithgirlz! CD Case
ISBN 0-310-81137-6

Faithgirlz! Backpack
ISBN 0-310-81228-3

Available now at your local bookstore!

faiThGirLz!
2 corinthians 4:18

Inner Beauty, Outward Faith

Now available from **inspirio**

Faithgirlz! Journal
ISBN 0-310-80713-1

Faithgirlz! Cross
ISBN 0-310-80715-8

The only thing that counts is faith expressing itself through love.
Galatians 5:6

A cheerful look brings joy to the heart.
Proverbs 15:30

Faithgirlz! Frame
ISBN 0-310-80714-X

Available now at your local bookstore!